KNIFE DEATH

Sundance's blade ripped open the front of Hunter's shirt, the knife tip making a thin red gash across his chest.

"Is that the best you can do, Sundance?" Hunter asked. "We've put on enough of a show. It's time to kill you."

And he put all his effort into trying. Their blades locked together, their tense sweating faces inches apart. But Sundance's heavy Bowie clanged hard against the handguard of Hunter's knife, and cut deeply into one of Hunter's fingers. When Hunter dropped his knife, Sundance was ready to finish him. But although Hunter had lost the knife in his right hand, Sundance had to deal with the derringer in his left...

BLOOD KNIFE

Jack Slade

LEISURE BOOKS • NEW YORK CITY

A LEISURE BOOK

Published by

Nordon Publications, Inc.
Two Park Avenue
New York, N.Y. 10016

1

Two men repairing a wall partially ruined by Apache fire arrows heard hoofbeats on the freight road and turned to look at the rider on a tall appaloosa.

One of the men, gaunt and suddenly pale, dropped his hammer and reached for a rifle. His companion said hurriedly, "That ain't no 'Pache. It's Jim Sundance, sure as hell."

His voice reached a tall, black-haired young man with the sharp features of the Indian. He was trying awkwardly to empty a pail of water off the veranda of a squat saloon. His white man's hat, the crown uncreased, rode like a gray dome atop his head. He stood with the thumb of his right hand hooked in his belt not as an affectation, but to anchor a nearly useless right arm.

Sundance approached the saloon on the great Nez Perce war horse Eagle, spring sunlight touching his weathered sombrero, red neckerchief, and fringed buckskin shirt. Long yellow hair brushed his shoulders.

"Eddie Strong," Sundance called as the young Cheyenne started for the side of the saloon, limping on the right leg. "Heard you were over here, Eddie. Rode twenty miles out of my way to make sure."

Sundance dismounted, standing tall in the moccasins he always wore instead of boots. He caught the young Cheyenne before he could get away and clasped the left hand in greeting, trying to hide the rage that sight of the ruined young man always kindled in him. "Finally caught up with you," Sundance said.

"You think you can talk me into going home," Strong said in Cheyenne, because the two carpenters at the stable next door were staring.

"One reason I'm here, Eddie, is for you to tell me about Burke Hunter. I may have found him at last."

"Why do you think I stay here in Arizona? Why do you think I came this far south in the first place? *Him!*"

"Describe Hunter. Everything you can remember about him."

"I told you. Two years ago. When it happened." Eddie, known as Two Clouds in the Cheyenne nation, looked bitterly at his right arm. "When I find him, I'll cut him worse than he cut me."

"No. Your father was my friend, like a father after mine was killed." Sundance spoke urgently, black eyes boring into the young man's face. "I'm the same as your guardian. You're to go back to our people."

"I've got a job here." Eddie Strong started away, limping badly.

Sundance halted him and jerked a thumb disdainfully at the squat saloon Eddie Strong was about to enter. "Swamping in a saloon is no job for a Cheyenne warrior."

"With this bad wing of mine and my leg, you call me a warrior?" Strong said bitterly.

"You can learn to shoot a rifle left handed. I told you that two years ago. You got away from me then. Not again, Eddie."

"Shoot what, Jim? White men? The buffalo are going fast."

"The buffalo will last," Jim Sundance said, mouth in coppery features tightening despite his attempt to sound convincing. Secretly he was not at all sure the Indian's main food supply, the buffalo, would survive the ambitions of those who sought to build their own empire on the ashes of the red man's. The scorched wall of the stable next door was a reminder. Weeks ago Apaches had attempted to burn it down along with the four other buildings in the town. The territory seethed since a massacre of Apache women and children by whites. It was not a year to try and rescue a white man being held prisoner by Apaches, yet Jim Sundance might try. He hadn't quite decided. Money was a consideration. In this case vengeance was more important. It depended on what he learned from Eddie Strong.

"Last time I was north I saw your chief," Sundance said. "I told him not to blame you because of what happened. You left the tribe because you wanted to try your wings. You got hurt by three unknown white men. In a knife fight."

"There was only one white man," Eddie Strong said bitterly. "I couldn't even handle *one* man. Let alone three."

"Sounds better the way I told it to your chief."

"What difference does it make?" Strong demanded.

"Because if I gave him the name of the bastard

who lured you into a knife fight and then crippled you the Cheyennes might take his trail." Sundance stared into the young man's eyes. "This one I want for myself, this Burke Hunter."

Eddie Strong shook his head, braided hair swinging out from beneath the high-domed sombrero. "He's here in Arizona. A freighter in Kansas told me he heard of a man here named Burke Hunter."

Sundance interrupted, stressing the realities of life on the frontier. Even if he bested a white man in a fair fight, the gallows would probably be his reward. An Indian kill a white man and go unpunished? Unthinkable.

Eddie Strong this year seemed more inclined to listen to reason than he had two years before in Newton, Kansas. He was tired, constantly harrassed by whites. Sundance finally got him to describe in detail his assailant in the knife fight. A man who, instead of backing off in victory, had deliberately severed tendons in right arm and leg.

Sundance listened gravely to Eddie Strong's emotion-packed voice describe his tragedy. "I want to be sure he's the Burke Hunter I'm looking for."

"Jim, you do know where he is." Eddie Strong seemed spent. "I'll fight him left-handed, damn it. All I want is another chance. I was a kid then. I'm smarter now. I can handle him."

"I'll handle him. You're going back to our people."

"Where is he, Jim? Tell me."

"Seems the Apaches have got him."

Eddie Strong looked surprised, then burst out laughing. "A prisoner? Of Apaches?"

"So they say."

Strong continued his almost hysterical laughter, drawing several men to saloon window and doors.

Then the young man was grim, no longer laughing. "I hope they give him the thousand cuts."

"An easy death compared to some they can give."

Eddie Strong looked intently at Sundance. "You going after him . . . in an Apache camp?" He sounded incredulous.

"If I find out for sure he's the same Burke Hunter who cut you."

"If he is," Eddie Strong interrupted quickly, "don't let him try and get you in a knife fight like he did me."

Sundance smiled coldly, letting his hand fall to the sheathed Bowie knife at his belt. "I'll try and remember your warning, Eddie."

"Jim, I mean it. I talked big a minute ago, but Hunter can cut you quicker than you can blink. Between the two of us we can handle him."

Sundance shook his head. "I want your promise to go home." It took more argument but finally Sundance prevailed. Strong gave his word, a sacred bond to an Indian, never given lightly.

"You got wages coming, Eddie?"

"Some," Eddie hedged.

"What do you mean, some?"

Eddie Strong seemed embarrassed to tell how a drunk had given him a shove. "My bad leg buckled and I fell over my bucket and the mop handle went through a side window. Hearne says I have to pay for it. But I don't know how much."

"Eddie, you get ready to travel."

Sundance entered the saloon. Some men had been staring out the window at the Appaloosa, Eagle, the Henry rifle in a saddle scabbard, a bedroll, and two bags made of buffalo hide. These contained weapons more primitive but as lethal in the deadly life game Sundance had chosen to play, when the Cheyenne blood in his veins prevailed over the white. Now the men turned to stare at Sundance's tall figure, awed by the golden hair in contrast to Cheyenne features. Of special interest was the Colt with ivory grips riding at his hip.

Hearne, a beefy, red-faced man, stared across his bar at Sundance and said roughly, "I don't sell whiskey to Indians. Not even to breeds."

"The whiskey you likely sell in a place like this I wouldn't feed to a snake."

Patrons gasped, some moving quickly away.

Hearne reddened, started to splutter, but Sundance told him why he was here. "I want Eddie Strong's wages due."

"I don't pay till the first of the month."

"He's going back to his people."

Hearne laughed, winked at some of those nearby. "If he's quittin', he gets *no* pay."

"I want every cent due him. And don't take out for that broken window. It wasn't his fault."

"You givin' me orders!" Hearne roared. "In me own saloon!"

One of the patrons shouted a warning. "Better go easy, Fred! That's *Jim Sundance*!"

"No goddam halfbreed's gonna tell me..." Hearne was reaching for a sawed-off shotgun under the bar when he found himself staring at the cold metal eye of the Colt Sundance had swiftly drawn. He licked his lips, then looked at the man who had shouted the warning. "You...you said Jim Sundance?" Hearne swallowed and turned back to Sundance. "I hear you take scalps. An' I sure don't figure to have mine hangin' at your belt."

"No scalps. Just the money you owe Eddie Strong."

Sundance reached across the bar with his left hand, and with the dozen or so stunned patrons looking on, he took the shotgun from Hearne's moist fingers. Only then did Sundance holster the Colt. He unloaded the shotgun, dropped the shells into a spittoon, then placed the shotgun on the bar.

Sundance watched carefully as Hearne, trembling slightly, placed several coins on the bartop. Sundance scooped them up, turned and warned the onlookers with his eyes, then walked out.

As the swing doors flapped at his back it seemed that everyone inside, including Hearne, gave an audible sigh of relief.

Sundance rode north five miles with Eddie Strong to make sure Hearne hadn't decided, with the help of friends, to try and get his money back.

He shook Eddie Strong's left hand and wished him well on his return to the Cheyennes.

"If you run into Burke Hunter," the younger man said in parting, "give him a lick for me."

"If he turns out to be the same Burke Hunter, he'll get more than that."

That evening in camp, Sundance reread Eloise Hunter's letter, which included directions to the ranch she and her missing husband owned. The letter, three weeks old, finally caught up with him in eastern Arizona where he had been doing some special work for one of his few friends in the cavalry, General Marcus Tyne.

> "Dear Mr. Sundance: It has been suggested that you are the only man who can possibly rescue my husband, Burke Hunter, from Apache brigands who are holding him pris-

oner. I will pay twenty thousand dollars the moment my husband is safe, plus a bonus we will decide on between us. If interested, contact Eloise Hunter, Mesa Seca, Terr. Arizona. May I expect you soon?
P.S. An acquaintance, Avery Pinder, recommends you highly."

Sundance restored the letter to a waterproof pouch and smiled grimly at gathering shadows. He was thinking of the missing husband. The trail of Burke Hunter over the past two years had been frustrating; Sundance had little time to devote to trying to run down the man who had crippled the son of an old friend. Now, however, it had been dropped in his lap. There was always the chance, of course, that this was a different Burke Hunter. And if so, the money alone, if everything was as the Hunter woman had claimed, was lure enough for such a risky undertaking as invading the territory of hostile Apaches.

Avery Pinder, whom the woman had mentioned, was now a Tucson merchant. Sundance had known him as a supplier for the railroad when tracks were pushing west. In five minutes of talk with Pinder, he could tell if the woman was lying about the twenty thousand dollars, and if her husband was the professional knife fighter he had been seeking these past two years. But he didn't want to waste time going all the way to Tucson to question Pinder about the woman.

And there was the chance that in the weeks since the letter had been written, Hunter had either been killed by his captors or freed.

Even if there was no longer money involved,

Hunter would pay for what he had so brutally done to Eddie Strong. Provided he was the same Hunter. Sundance had a hunch that he was.

2

His first glimpse of the Hunter horse ranch was disappointing. There were a few cottonwoods overhanging a small house, a barn, two sheds, and some two dozen head of horses in a pasture. Such an outfit didn't look substantial enough to produce the twenty thousand dollar fee mentioned by Eloise Hunter. This part of it he guessed was already a lie. Perhaps his only payment would be vengeance for Eddie Strong, although he was beginning to wonder if a famous knife fighter and well-known philanderer would settle down with a wife on such a nondescript ranch.

He glanced again at the horses. Good ones, from what he could see. He wondered if horse flesh so important to the Indian for survival in the increasingly hostile white world was the reason Apaches had taken Hunter prisoner. Did they capture him and some of his horses in payment for some past wrong done their people? The mere fact that the Hunter ranch was on land where the Apaches had once roamed free was reason enough in the Indian mind.

This Sundance could well understand, for he lived with his feet planted firmly in two worlds, Indian and white.

Nearing the house, he saw for the first time two spent saddle horses in the cottonwoods by the house, a squat structure of adobe with a flat roof of brush. The two horses stood hipshot, heads down, giving the appearance of having been ridden hard and fast, the owners so eager to reach the house they had not even bothered to tether the animals to a tie rack only a few feet away nor to loosen cinches. Riders in a hell of a hurry, Sundance thought. He instinctively eased the ivory-butted Colt in its holster.

For the first time he was aware of a drone of voices, one of them a woman's, coming from the house. He listened intently but could make out nothing that was being said. One of the weary horses whinnied at the sight of Eagle. Sundance tensed, swung down and drew his Colt, waiting for some indication from the house that the horse had alerted its occupants.

The voices from the house grew louder and then a woman suddenly screamed in terror. "Please! How many times do I have to say that I can't tell you what I don't know!"

A man answered harshly. "Burke told you where the mine was. You know damn well he did."

"Hatch, I don't even know that it is a mine."

"Don't lie, Eloise!"

"He didn't say *what* it was, Hatch."

"But he showed you nuggets."

"He . . . he told me about them . . ." The woman

sounded frantic. "But I don't know where he got them!" she cried as Sundance crept closer to the house. He saw an open window off a narrow veranda, curtains blowing in the faint breeze.

A man with a high-pitched voice and a giggle asked, "Mrs, Hunter, ma'am, you gonna say them nuggets come from the moon?"

"A mine," a third man said angrily. Sundance had thought at first there were only two men in the house, those who had ridden up on the spent horses. Obviously there was at least one more.

"You got a map of that mine, Eloise," the voice of Hatch persisted, a smoother, slightly more cultured voice than the other two.

"Hatch, if there *is* a map, my husband has it with him!"

The one with the deep voice was skeptical. "Look, ma'am, me an' Clyde rode damn fast to get here. When Hatch never sent us word like he said he would, we figured it was time to do it our way."

"Damn it, Chaney," Hatch said, "I told you it'd take time."

"You had time enough to soft soap ten wimmen, let alone only one. So keep out of it, Hatch. You had your turn. Now it's ours. Ma'am, you listen close. We know your husband had a sack of nuggets. Bragged that they was only a drop in the bucket. Now a man with a mine rich as that would sure as hell tell his wife where it is an' leave her a map, in case somethin' happened to him. Which is damn well likely happened already, knowin' them 'Paches like I do."

Sundance moved soundlessly in his moccasins along the veranda as the woman began to cry.

Which prompted Hatch to say, "I told you it wouldn't do any good to yell at her, Chaney."

"You an' your charm," Chaney scoffed. "Hell, we give you rope enough to get to her with honey. Now we'll try vinegar."

"You've ruined it, Chaney. Another day and I'd have had her seeing things our way . . ."

"Another day, hell!" the deep-voiced Chaney shouted. "With all we got on our heads, Mexico's the only safe place."

"Then let's take her with us," Hatch said.

Chaney ignored him. "Clyde, how's that spike comin'?"

"Gettin' hot," Clyde giggled.

The woman screamed. "Hatch, don't let them hurt me!"

"Then tell us what you know about that mine."

"Burke wouldn't think enough of me to tell me anything," she whimpered. "You must believe me. You *must!*"

"That spike gettin' hotter, Clyde?" Chaney asked casually.

"Almost red."

Eloise Hunter sobbed. "Please, please, you're not fiends . . . only Indians are the fiends. Surely not white men . . ."

Sundance, approaching the narrow window, stiffened at the woman's word. Fiends, she calls us, he thought. Yet in her letter she had desperately sought his aid. The window was too narrow, little more than a rifle port; heavy shutters cut off his view of the interior. The shutters had been slammed shut, trapping one of the lace curtains.

"Hatch, don't *let* them . . ." She was babbling in fear.

Clyde giggled and said in his high-pitched voice, "When your husband gets home, he'll be some s'prised to find our initials branded on your chest."

"Surely you *wouldn't*!" Eloise Hunter cried.

Colt drawn, Sundance moved past a heavy door that was closed, then on toward a window, this one wider than the first.

"Handle that spike careful, Clyde," Chaney advised. "Better have a good grip on them pliers. Now, Mrs. Hunter, one last chance. You come up with a map or you take us to the mine. Either one."

"But I don't know where it is!"

Sundance reached the wider window. It was open, the inner shutters not closed. Lacy curtains stirred in the same hot afternoon breeze that dried sweat on the back of his neck. He looked into the house at a big parlor-kitchen. They were at the far end, next to a stove. The woman, tall and pretty, was backed up to a heavy table. Her dress was green, torn at the shoulder. Thick auburn hair was tumbling from its pins. She was obviously terrified of the three men who had their backs to Sundance, their attention on the woman.

Sundance squeezed soundlessly through the window, avoiding overturned furniture; drawers emptied. A metal box pried open. A stocky man was gripping her left arm. A slender red-headed man with a thick mustache had her other arm.

The third man, Clyde, towering and black-bearded, was using a pair of pliers to pick up a hot spike from a bed of coals in the cook stove. He giggled, and it seemed strange for such a large man. He moved toward her, the glowing point aimed at her chest.

The stocky Chaney said, "Ma'am, it looks like it'll take a hot iron to loosen your tongue." He reached out a heavy hand to rip down the front of her green dress.

"Let's see some bare skin," Clyde said.

And at that instant the woman glimpsed Sundance. Her already terrified features collapsed completely. Eyes rolled back in her head, the jaw dropping.

But just before she passed out she did manage to scream, *"Apaches!"*

The one dreaded word was all it took to produce instant chaos. Clyde spun around, dropping the pliers and hot nail to the stone floor. He made a grab for a big cedar-butted gun at his belt. Large yellowish teeth behind the tangle of beard presented a target.

Sundance's first shot in that moment of pandemonium smashed them and exited at the base of the skull, the snarl of surprise still on lips now bloodied. Clyde toppled to the floor, one cheek pressed against the hot spike intended to have been used as a branding iron on the woman now sprawled in a dead faint. The two men who had been holding her by the arms, Hatch and Chaney, had leaped aside. In those few seconds, Sundance noticed that the tall, red-mustached Hatch was bootless, wearing only heavy socks on his feet. Hatch squeezed off a shot, the bullet chipping into adobe at Sundance's back and ricocheting. And then, echoing the woman's cry of "Apaches," he flung himself headfirst out the nearest open window.

But Sundance's attention was on Chaney, a chunky, tense-looking man in a plaid shirt that appeared to be brand new. As Chaney thumb-cocked a revolver, Sundance shot him twice through the plaids of the shirt. Chaney fell backward, his weight splintering a chair. His wild shot fanned Sundance's earlobe and punched an asterisk in the front door.

Sounds of a horse pushed suddenly into a hard

run. Sundance jerked open the front door and glimpsed Hatch in wild flight, disappearing into the cottonwoods. Sundance let him go. His Henry rifle would have brought down the fleeing rider, but with the Colt it was unlikely. He reloaded, the pounding hoofbeats fading rapidly.

Quickly he disarmed the two men crumpled on the floor, although in Clyde's case there was no need. The pulpy back of his head attested to that. The heavy-set Chaney clung to a reed of life, but barely. Air in the room was heavy with the sharp odor of cordite and with smears of powdersmoke blending into a haze.

Sundance dragged the dead Clyde through the litter of papers and overturned furniture and to the yard. When he returned to the house Eloise Hunter was still unconscious.

A gasp of surprise caused Sundance to wheel. Chaney, pale as the death that approached so remorselessly, stared in awe from the floor. "You ain't no 'Pache . . ."

"Cheyenne," Sundance grunted, staring down at the dying man without compassion.

"You Cheyenne? With that yaller hair?"

"Fools a lot of people. I'm also white. Although it's seeing the likes of you that sometimes makes me ashamed to admit it."

Sundance picked up Eloise Hunter from the floor and carried her to the single bedroom. A heavy drape at the window cut out most of the sunlight. He lowered her gently to a rumpled bed. Stepping back, he saw a pair of boots belonging to a man, thrown carelessly half under the bed. He also noticed a still-smouldering cigar atop a chest of drawers. It had burned a groove in the polished wood.

Returning to the front room, he saw that Chaney

had squirmed about on his buttocks, leaving a trail of blood on the stone floor. "Look, there's gold... millions in gold," he babbled. "Make the woman tell where it is an' we'll go halves."

"How do you know about millions?"

Chaney started to speak and then life flickered out. Sundance dragged him to the yard and left him by a shed wall next to Clyde's body. It made no sense to waste time digging graves; he'd have to notify the law in the nearest town, which was Mesa Seca. And the deputy there would want to see the bodies.

Glimpsing a face at the window, Sundance knew it was Eloise Hunter. Thinking in her panic she might grab a gun, he sprinted for the house. He found her hunched in a chair, still numb from shock.

"You... you gave me such a fright," she whispered.

"You gave them more than that when you yelled 'Apaches'."

"You're Jim Sundance, of course. I might have known. Avery Pinder described you when he was through here last month." She looked at the blood streaks on the floor and shuddered. "Where are they? What happened to them?"

"To the happy hunting ground, as my white brethren like to call it."

"Are they *all* dead?"

He told her that the bootless one known as Hatch had got away. "Now that you're conscious, maybe I'd better run him down. I didn't want to leave you alone."

"No... no..." She seemed flustered. "He's quite dangerous they say... a gunman..."

"In other words you don't *want* me to go after him."

She was staring with a certain morbid fascination

at the spike and pliers on the floor, the auburn hair disheveled. But her green eyes were losing their terror.

"Hatch deserves the worst," Sundance said when she made no reply. "After what he and the other two were planning."

"I . . . I don't really think they'd have harmed me. Try to scare me to death, yes. And they came close to doing that."

"They meant business. Who are they, anyhow?"

"Hatch has . . . has been helping out here at the ranch. Since my husband was captured. I never saw Clyde and Chaney before."

He had to admire her resilience; her voice had lost its hysteria and she seemed reasonably calm after experiencing such obvious terror.

Sundance said coolly, "I guess Chaney and Clyde showing up here got Hatch so upset he forgot to put on his boots."

She met his gaze boldly. "He was taking a nap. He has been working very hard . . . Don't look at me like that. It's the truth."

I wonder just how much truth is in you, lady, he wanted to say.

He glanced at some of the papers strewn over the floor. Shares in a riverboat. Stock certificates from a railroad Sundance knew was defunct.

"Tell me, Mrs. Hunter," he said bluntly, "how do you *know* your husband is a prisoner of the Apaches?"

"Burke wrote to me. The letter was smuggled out of the Apache camp. I can tell you it frightened me half to death when I realized an Apache could come right up to the door and leave a letter. Without me hearing him . . ."

"And what did the letter say?" Sundance asked skeptically.

"It said that I should get hold of Jim Sundance. That he should come to the camp and rescue him. That he was the only one who could do it. Some way Burke knew you were here in Arizona."

"Let me see the letter. The one you say an Apache left on your doorstep."

She missed the irony. "I gave it to Hatch to read. He... he never returned it." She brushed back her auburn hair, her mouth suddenly tight. "Don't look at me like that, Jim Sundance. I am not lying." She bent her head. Tears made damp spots on the lap of the green dress. At least the tears seemed genuine. "After that Apache left Burke's letter I... I just couldn't stay out here alone. I hired Hatch. And yes, he knew Clyde and Chaney all right. I found that out today."

"There really is a gold mine?"

"Burke had nuggets with him the last time he was home. Worth thousands of dollars."

"Might've been fool's gold."

She shook her head. "Grimholdt saw them. He's the assayer in Mesa Seca. You can ask him."

"Don't worry, I will." Sundance righted some of the overturned furniture, then said casually, "Was ransom mentioned in the letter?"

"Not a hint."

Something was wrong, but he couldn't quite tell what it was.

She went to a window and stared out at Eagle who had wandered nearer the house to crop grass. "What a spendid animal. What do you call it?"

He told her.

"A fitting name, Eagle," she said, turning to give

him a warm smile. "And your name is also fitting. Sundance. I like it. An unusual name."

"A name the Cheyennes gave my father. He was English."

"And your mother?"

"Smiling Woman of the Cheyennes."

"You see them occasionally, of course."

"They were killed."

"Oh, I'm sorry. How did they die?"

"Something I never talk about," he answered angrily.

"No need to take my head off. I was merely curious."

"Why hasn't the cavalry gone looking for your husband? It's what usually happens when somebody is captured by Indians."

She said that her husband had stressed in his letter that no one was to be notified, especially the military. "Only Jim Sundance. It seems terribly important that you go to where he is being held prisoner."

"And where is that?"

"Honestly I don't know."

"Don't play me for a fool, Mrs. Hunter," he warned coldly. He mentioned the boots in the bedroom and the cigar that had burned its own brand into the chest of drawers. He told her of the things he had overheard, the late Chaney's reference to honey and vinegar.

For a moment her green eyes snapped and he waited for her to say, "How dare you," but she had too much good sense for that.

"Don't try and tell me there's no boots or cigar. You likely got rid of them while I was outside. If you didn't you're a bigger fool than I think you are."

"A fool I am not!" She leaped at him and tried to claw his face in her spilling rage, but he pinioned both her wrists in one large hand. When he felt a sharp pain at his shin from the pointed toe of her boot, he thrust her roughly aside.

"Look. Mrs. Hunter, I don't give a damn about you and that Hatch. You offered me a business proposition in your letter. And I happened to get here in time to keep your pretty flesh from getting branded. Those three hombres would as soon cut your heart out as shake your hand. I know their type. And that includes your friend Hatch."

She drew a deep breath, shoulders back so that her rather splendid breasts were even more pronounced under the green dress. "I am relieved to hear you say that you're going to help me." In the deepening shadows she was even more handsome.

"I didn't say for sure I'd help, Mrs. Hunter. I need a few more details."

"There's so much I don't know about the gold . . ."

"Details mainly about your husband. There was a Burke Hunter in Kansas. A knife fighter. Your husband the same one?"

"Why is that important?" she demanded, wary.

"I just like to know who I'm dealing with."

"Oh. Well, Burke is a marvel with a knife. He brags about it often. But his talk of cold steel always makes me shiver."

Sundance bared his teeth. "So he *is* the one."

"What do you mean by that?"

"Burke Hunter, knife fighter. I just wanted to make sure."

Sundance was taking another tour of the windows when she said, "If you're worried about Hatch, I doubt if he'll be back for his boots." She sounded faintly bitter. "He's rich enough to have more than one pair. He probably thinks half the Apaches in the territory swarmed in on the house from the way I screamed. I'll tell you the truth about Hatch. I met him in town. He said he was a friend of Burke's and offered to help me out here. With Burke gone I just couldn't manage. And I thought you were going to ignore my letter."

"Frontier's a big place. Took awhile to reach me."

"I guess Hatch was after the gold. I was so upset by Burke missing and all the rest of it that I didn't realize it. And then just before you got here Chaney and that other one, that Clyde, came pounding in. As if somebody might be after them, a sheriff or marshal." She looked up at him, her eyes softening. "Hatch seemed to think that there'll be another letter from Burke any day. Telling where he is being held. Hatch said it's only logical."

"Maybe another letter did come. And he didn't bother showing it to you. After all, he doesn't give a damn about your husband. Only the gold."

"What do you give a damn about, Jim Sundance?" she asked softly.

He destroyed her mood by telling her bluntly that she should stay at the nearest town until he could find her husband in the Apache camp. She didn't like the idea, but he persisted and she finally admitted the wisdom of the suggestion. With so much money at stake there was no telling who might strike out at her next.

"I could stay with a woman friend, a widow," Eloise, said thoughtfully. "Another day or so won't make any difference, however."

"We leave now."

"Surely not till morning. It won't make any difference to Burke whether you get started in one day or three. He's already been gone over a month."

Sundance sensed there was more to it than Burke Hunter being captured by Apaches. If Apaches even had him as captive. It was debatable. "Maybe the Apaches took him as a whim," Sundance said, watching her face. "Maybe it goes deeper. Maybe he was violating their territory with his gold mine. And that's serious business these days to an Indian. We're getting pushed into smaller and smaller corners."

"You talk like an Indian, Sundance."

"I am one. Half of me, at least."

"Yes, of course, a magnificent Indian."

He looked her over. Now that he had calmed down after being thrown into a sudden gun battle that had claimed two lives, she was even more appealing. But there were too many loose ends here; he had no intention of committing himself just yet.

That business of Hunter smuggling a letter out of an Apache camp, suggesting his wife contact Jim Sundance, sounded strange. Of course this Burke Hunter might have heard of him and knew he had had contact with Apaches in other years. But why was the letter conveniently in the possession of the bootless Hatch?

Eloise said, "If the Apaches have forced Burke to tell them the location of the mine, I'm sure you can get that information. You're one of them, or almost. As you just reminded me." Her dazzling smile reminded him of the bonus she had mentioned in her letter. Time enough to collect, if and when.

"Which is it you want most, Mrs. Hunter?" he drawled. Your husband or a map of that mine?"

"Both," she answered, looking him in the eye.

"But you want one a little more than the other, eh?"

By the time they reached Mesa Seca, the widow,

Leticia Dorn, had already retired. But she opened the door of a rambling one-story adobe house in answer to Eloise Hunter's knock. The woman was tall and quite thin and obviously embarrassed that Sundance was seeing her gray hair done up in curly rags.

After the widow had gone off to a bedroom, Sundance issued instructions to Eloise. She was to have on hand several sheets of writing paper and pen and ink by the time he returned in the morning.

"For what purpose?" she demanded in her imperious manner.

"If everything is as you say, then I'm going to write out a contract. I'll expect payment in full, Mrs. Hunter."

"You had a chance for the first payment out at the ranch," she said in a fierce whisper. "But you insisted on bringing me here."

"For your own safety."

"I'm beginning to wonder if you're not a certain kind of Indian that Burke told me about once," she said scornfully. "Young males, when they reach a certain age, are allowed to decide which they want, life as a warrior or life as a woman."

Sundance's smile was cold. "They are considered sacred and free to live as they choose, these half men—half women. I am not one of them."

"Well, you act as if you don't want a woman," she said, finally blushing under his steady gaze, "only money. So I thought there must be something wrong with you."

"Or maybe something wrong with you."

Her green eyes flashed. "Just what do you mean?"

"I'm pretty particular, Mrs. Hunter. I've loved women for pay, sure. I'll do it again before I die. But

I've never yet let a female put a ring in my nose. So we run things my way. Or not at all. It's up to you."

She seethed for a moment, and then it all seemed to drain suddenly. "Damn you," she whispered. "All right, I'll agree to whatever you say. What else can I do?"

He reminded her to have paper, pen and ink on hand. He also suggested she arrange for someone to care for the horses at the ranch.

"See you in the morning," he said.

"Not even a kiss to bind it?"

"Later." And he knew that if he was forced to kill her husband, she might reward him not only with a kiss but much more. Out of gratitude? Or she might try to drive a knife blade into his belly as he held her. It all depended on how she really felt about Burke Hunter.

3

Sundance prowled the town in the early evening, looking for signs of the bootless Hatch, lone survivor of the shootout at the Hunter ranch, but saw no sign of the man. He found a sheriff's office and a one-cell jail, neither occupied. A saddlemaker just closing up shop next door said that the town's only representative of the law, a deputy sheriff, was at the other end of the county and wasn't expected back for several days.

Sundance thanked the man. With the deputy out of town, there was nothing to do but ride the three miles back to the Hunter ranch. Fortunately, moonlight was faint and provided cover, but tomorrow it would be full. Something he had to remember. Leaving Eagle away from the house, he approached on foot, deep shadows offering cover. But no one challenged him, no muzzle fire spitting from the darkness. He entered the house through a window, lit a lamp, turned the wick low and began a systematic search. But he found nothing. He got a shovel from a shed, dug two shallow graves, and buried the two scum who had intended to brand a woman with a red hot spike.

He returned to town where he nursed a whiskey in a saloon that held only a handful of patrons. He casually asked a thin, bald bartender if he knew a man called Hatch, and described him.

"He's the fella who went to work for Eloise Hunter," the man said. But he knew nothing of his background.

But when Sundance mentioned the other two, the eyes narrowed. "Clyde Stanhope an' Chaney Blake. They was in here two, three days ago, come to think of it. They got kinda drunk an' was threatenin' to shoot the place up. I was about to slip out an' go get ol' Hank, the deputy. But right then they must've figured what I was aimin' to do. They lit out. Next mawnin' I seen wanted notices out for them two in Hank's office. Thousand dollars reward on each of 'em. Hank's over east tryin' to run 'em down."

The bartender was called away to wait on a customer. Sundance had his second drink as the place began to fill up, drinking all the whiskey he ever allowed himself at one time.

The bartender finally came back, a puzzled look on his thin face. "Been thinkin' it over," he said. "Damn if I don't remember seein' Hatch talkin' to them two out behind the livery barn that same day. Reckon somebody better get word out to Mrs. Hunter that the fella she hired is hangin' out with a pair of killers. At least he knows 'em, that's for sure. He was joshin' with 'em and all..."

"Is Hatch a first or last name?" Sundance asked.

"Don't rightly know. But I do recollect a fella

askin' him in here one night when he drove Eloise in to do some shoppin' at the store. Hatch's face got almost as red in the face as his mustache, damn if he didn't."

"Just because the man asked about his name?"

"Yeah. Fella shoulda knowed better than to ask questions. But still an' all, Hatch did get awful riled over somethin' as simple as a fella wantin' to know was Hatch his first or last name."

Sundance, remembering the letter Eloise Hunter said had been left on her doorstep, wore a half-smile when he asked, "Any Apaches been seen around here lately?"

"An' injun show his face around here, he's dead quick." Then the bartender looked up at Sundance's coppery Cheyenne features, gulped and said hastily, "Full bloods, I mean. Halfbreeds is always welcome." This he said lamely. "Only other fella with injun blood been around here lately is Big Luke. But he . . ."

"This Luke part Apache?" Sundance asked narrowly.

"Part Navajo, I hear. Mean as he is big. But he don't show hisself much. Army's lookin' for him. Used to scout for Colonel Bixler. Army was gonna hang him for murder. But he got away." The barkeep leaned bony elbows on the bar and said confidentially, "I do recollect seein' Big Luke kill a fella over at Simon Springs 'bout two year back. Hit the poor bastard so hard in the gut with his fist that it busted everything loose inside."

Sundance casually asked about Grimholdt, the town's assayer. "Solid as a rock." Which didn't mean a hell of a lot, Sundance had learned from experience.

The bartender got busy, finished at least for the present as a source of information. Sundance decided to forego the lamp-lighted cafe down the block where he would be an easy target for an assassin. He ate the last of cold buffalo tongue, then stabled Eagle. The night hostler at the livery barn accepted an extra dollar for information, and a second one for allowing Sundance to bed down in the hay.

The hostler knew even less than the bartender about the fugitive from the gallows, Big Luke. But he did recall Chaney and Clyde when Sundance described them. They had put up their horses in the stable one night and had a long, low-voiced conference in the wagonyard out back, with the man known as Hatch. Hatch was working out at the Hunter ranch, the hostler confided. And no, he hadn't seen Chaney and Clyde since.

And you won't see them now, Sundance felt like adding. Ever again.

Sundance felt it was just as well that the deputy sheriff was out of town. That he was off chasing the two men Sundance had killed was ironic. This way Sundance could get on with unravelling the mystery of Burke Hunter's disappearance without possible delay, while a small town deputy investigated the deaths of the pair.

And there was always the possibility Eloise Hunter might decide to tell a different version, Sundance thought, reflecting on an old adage concerning "a woman scorned." There was also Hatch, who had fled the scene and might have his own version. With no deputy around, Sundance had an excuse not to report the killings.

Sundance studied the night hostler's freckled face

in the glare of a night lantern hanging on a post. "Speaking of the Hunter ranch, I hear Hunter himself hasn't been seen around lately."

"Some say the 'Paches took him," the garrulous hostler laughed. "More'n likely he's off somewhere with a female. He'll come back when he's had his fill, like he always does."

Sundance made his bed far back in a hay mow, Colt and Henry rifle at hand. He could have taken a room at the hotel next to the saloon, but he wanted to be near Eagle in case he had to hit the saddle. Not only did he have Hatch to worry about, but other possible friends of the two dead ones as well. And the name of the former Army scout, Big Luke, rolled around in his head. There was no reason for it except pure hunch that the man just might be trying to horn in on the Burke Hunter game of gold.

His presence in town in broad daylight the next morning caused much comment. Men on the walks stared at his yellow hair and women seemed startled by his tall figure, the Cheyenne features. Some of them went pale, no doubt having fresh memories of Indian troubles. A few of the younger ones stared first in amazement, then with interest, eyes glowing. He barely noticed, having more pressing matters in mind on that spring morning.

He ate steak and eggs at a cafe counter, delaying the finish of his breakfast until he could see that the assay office across the street was open for business. At last, through the dusty front window, he saw a plump man in a narrow brimmed hat and black suit key open the door of the small frame building on the corner.

Sundance paid for his meal, then crossed to the assay office and introduced himself to Cyrus

Grimholdt. The assayer seemed grumpy until he learned that his visitor's business concerned the missing Burke Hunter.

"If you're here to help Eloise, then I bid you welcome," Grimholdt said, looking him over through his eyeglasses. He waved Sundance to a chair behind a glass case containing labeled ore samples and seated himself at a rolltop desk.

When Sundance bluntly asked about the gold mine Hunter supposedly found, Grimholdt shook his head, saying such matters were confidential.

"Maybe I better ask how come you're mixed up in this, Sundance," Grimholdt said. "I want to help Eloise, but . . ." He spread pudgy hands wide from his body.

Sundance decided to show him the letter from Eloise Hunter, pleading for his help. And when Grimholdt scanned it, lips pursed, Sundance said that the woman was staying in town for the present and could verify the letter if necessary.

"Wasn't questioning the validity of the letter." Grimholdt's dark eyes searched Sundance's face. "I know Eloise's handwriting. It's just that a pretty woman in trouble is sometimes prey to scalawags. Hasn't been easy for Eloise, being married to Hunter."

"Not easy in what way?" Sundance sat where he had one eye on the street. A freight wagon was being unloaded in front of a store; women congregated on a street corner, talking. Riders came and went. He saw no sign of the red-mustached Hatch.

"Hunter's away from home sometimes months at a time, prospecting," Grimholdt said grimly. "Leaves her alone out at the ranch. Burke Hunter's been hell-bent to find a mine he says has been lost since conquistador days. Or so he once confided when he'd had more whiskey than was good for him." Grimholdt gave a short laugh. "Yeah, I'm talking more than I ever do. But my daughter and Eloise went to school together for a time and I remember her folks."

"You think he found that old mine?"

"Seems like it," the assayer admitted. "But don't know what good it'll do if the Apaches have got him, as Eloise claims in her letter. I know he's been gone, but I didn't know where."

"I heard he might not be a captive at all, but using it as an excuse to be off somewhere with a woman."

"I know those rumors going around. But this time I think it's gold, not a woman. Hunter showed me some nuggets last time he was here."

Sundance leaned forward. "Yes?"

"He didn't let me look at all of them. Only a few. The ones he showed me were worth close to seventy thousand. With the others he had in that sack he had to have at least a hundred thousand that day." Grimholdt gave a deep sigh. "I've seen some strikes in my time but this was incredible. I guess we all dream of stumbling onto riches. But seems as if Hunter made it come true."

"How many people know about this?"

"Don't rightly know." Grimholdt seemed suddenly embarrassed. "Maybe that fella Hatch working out at the ranch. A woman alone a lot of the time . . . well, she might weaken and tell things to a fella that she wouldn't even think of if her husband was home where he should be." The last he said strongly.

"You tell anybody about Hunter's find?"

Grimholdt shook his head. "He paid me for my

services, and I feel ethically bound not to talk. About the same as the doctor with his patient, if you know what I mean. But here I am talking to you." He shook his head. "But I do worry about Eloise."

"You talk about ethics. Not many men feel like you do. Talk of a gold strike usually loosens the tongue even faster than whiskey."

Grimholdt hitched his chair around. "I might as well tell you the rest of it. Si Devlon swears he saw Hunter captured by Apaches."

"Devlon? Who's he?"

"Got a mine north of here. In Apache country."

"He must either be a fool or he has more guts than an elephant."

"Probably the latter," Grimholdt said with a wry smile. "They've let him alone so far." Grimholdt said that Devlon was usually close-mouthed. "But he'll talk to me whenever I run an assay on ore samples he brings in. Eloise happened to be here when he was telling his story about the Apaches. But she begged me not to say anything more about it. She seemed afraid the cavalry would get wind of it and go charging off to the mountains. And that the Apaches would kill her husband just for spite. I don't know why she worries about him. He never did much for her."

"What happened to the nuggets Hunter had with him?"

Grimholdt removed brass framed eyeglasses and stared out the window, frowning. "He said he was going to hide half the nuggets out at the ranch. Said he had a special place nobody would ever think of looking. I advised him to leave the nuggets here in my safe. But he ignored me. I did ask him to promise to tell Eloise where he would hide them, in case anything happened to him. But whether he did or not, I have no way of knowing."

Sundance was remembering that Eloise Hunter had said nothing about nuggets.

Grimholdt said, "Hunter had those nuggets with him when he left for the ranch. He was there a few days and then returned to the mountains. That's when the Apaches jumped him, according to Si Devlon."

"You sure about this Devlon?"

"He's devious. He'll try to get money out of you if you want information. So be prepared. But I do believe that in the long run his word is solid gold. Even if his prospects for finding much at that two bit mine aren't."

"Where can I find this Devlon?"

Grimholdt got pencil and paper and drew a map. "Just be sure and let him know you come as a friend. He's built a regular fortress out there. And he's a dead shot."

Sundance decided to tell Grimholdt about the gunfight. When he had finished, the assayer paled. "Thank God you persuaded Eloise to move to town."

"I buried those two," Sundance said thinly. "Tell the deputy when he gets back. If I get through this business alive, I'll answer his questions."

Grimholdt was thoughtfully rubbing his jaw. "Been chewing it over in my mind, and from the way you describe those men you killed, they're probably Chaney Blake and Clyde Stanhope. Miners cover a lot of territory out here and they tell me things they don't even repeat in a saloon. Your friends . . . your late friends . . . Chaney and Clyde, are wanted in New Mexico. And you say Hatch is in with them?

Lordy, when he went out there to give Eloise a hand, I only thought that at last she'd have a man to help out. And he and the other two were only sniffing gold dust, as Si Devlon likes to put it. The bastards. I'm glad you killed those two. If I see Hatch in town again I'll get some of my friends and we'll hold him for the sheriff."

Sundance stood up. "By the way, you know anything about a half-breed former scout calling himself Big Luke?"

Grimholdt could add nothing to what Sundance had learned last night. "Might be he's tied himself in with one of the Apache chiefs," the assayer went on gravely. He spoke of the massacre some months ago of Apache women and children by whites and others. "Things have been worse since. I know some of the Apaches have pulled away from Cochise. One of the medicine men has got them stirred up because of the massacre. I hear Colonel Bixler's off chasing Cochise."

"So I understand," Sundance said, turning for the door.

"A sorry business, you ask me, when human beings of different color and cultures can't live in peace without murdering each other."

"Maybe this sorry business will end one day . . . soon."

"You've heard something in the wind that I don't know about?"

Sundance shrugged; he had his own plan, known only to a few. It was something he couldn't talk about.

He thanked Grimholdt for his information. "Now let's see if I can find Burke Hunter." He shoved the map Grimholdt had drawn into his pants pocket.

"Whenever you mention Eloise's husband, your voice has an edge."

Sundance's smile was cold.

"Eloise is sometimes a fool where men are concerned," Grimholdt explained gravely. "She was with Burke Hunter. My wife and I tried to talk her out of marrying him. Turns me cold whenever I'd see him show off with that knife of his and brag."

"He cut a friend of mine. One reason I'm going after him."

"Not for the money alone?"

"Not for the money alone."

Grimholdt squinted through his glasses. "I've heard about you for some years now. But everyone always says you hire out for money. Big money. Nothing else. This time it's different, eh?"

"Somewhat." Sundance was anxious to move on.

"Usually I don't hold with divorce, but in Eloise's case I make an exception. She's worked hard out at the ranch. Left alone most of the time. Hard to keep a crew, because whenever Hunter does decide to come home from his prospecting he's in a jealous rage and fires them all." Grimholdt looked at him steadily. "With her husband gone more than he's home, I don't blame Eloise for anything she might do. It's nobody's damn business."

Sundance met the piercing dark gray eyes. "I agree."

They parted with a firm handshake and Grimholdt's prayer for success.

At the home of the widow, Leticia Dorn, Sundance confronted Eloise in the parlor. He told her that Grimholdt had told him about nuggets. "Did your husband hide some of them at the ranch?"

"I . . . I don't remember . . ."

"This is no kid's game we're playing, Mrs. Hunter. I've had to kill two men already. God knows how many more before this thing is over and done."

She swallowed; the widow was in the back part of the house. "Burke left me a handful of the nuggets. I hid them. They're in a safe place."

"At the ranch?" He gave a bark of laughter. "You call that safe?"

"Nobody would ever think to look where they're hidden." She tossed back the long auburn hair that she had been brushing when he arrived. Her dress was light blue with a lacy collar. "If you hadn't been in such a hurry to leave the ranch, I might have told you about the nuggets."

"Might have?" he said wryly.

"But you had to have things your own way."

"If Hatch and those other scum had any idea you had nuggets hidden there you'd have had worse than a branding iron. Until you told them the hiding place."

Her grip tightened on the black-handled hair brush she was holding. "In about another minute I'd have blurted it out. About the nuggets. Anything to get them to leave me alone."

"They wouldn't have stopped with that. They'd kill their own mothers for one of those nuggets. Let alone a handful."

He bluntly stated it was time to get down to business. She led him to a dining room table where the items he had asked for were spread out. He sat down, dipped a pen, and began writing out his contract with Eloise Hunter. In this room with its uncurtained windows he could see her puffy eyes, lines of fatigue at mouth corners as if she'd slept poorly.

She caught him looking at her and said, "In the middle of the night it all came back to me." She shuddered. "Out at the ranch I could pretend to myself that they wouldn't have gone through with their plans. But I knew better. If you hadn't come when you did, there's no telling what might have happened to me."

He did not look up from his work.

She said, "Hatch seemed charming at first and I thought . . ." Her voice was bitter. "But so was Burke when I married him."

His pen scratching across the paper was the only sound in the room for several minutes. She watched him write, and as others had in the past, she marveled at the lines of precise copperplate he spread across the pages.

"Strange that a savage has such talents?" he said with a short laugh.

"You must admit it's unusual in a man who could beat two ruffians at their own game. And send a third running for his life."

"They thought it was Apaches. That helped."

"Don't underestimate your ability, Sundance . . . in anything."

He looked up, meeting the challenge of green eyes, then continued with his work. He made two copies of the contract. Then he sipped coffee the widow Dorn had brewed for him while Eloise read and reread the contract.

"A lawyer couldn't have put it better," Eloise said. "But there was no need to go to so much trouble. My word is good."

"When there's this much money at stake, everything's got to be set down in black and white."

Her lips curled as she watched him there at the

table, big and bronzed, black eyes glinting in sunlight streaming through a side window. "Then you admit your own word isn't worth much," she snapped.

"It is."

"Do tell me why," she said mockingly.

"It's my Cheyenne blood." He stood up, towering over her. "I'll need your signature on those papers. And your friend the widow as witness."

"And then what?" she demanded.

"I'll do my damndest to find your husband.

"And don't forget his map of the mine."

"Get it over his dead body if I have to."

She met his cold smile, then went to the kitchen. "Letty, would you witness my signature, please?"

Her voice, Sundance noticed, was unsteady.

4

There was no deadlier stretch of territory on the frontier than that which Sundance was crossing by noontime. Conditions had been bad enough due to promises made by the whites and then callously disregarded. But the greatest treachery to the Apaches had been directed at one of their chiefs, Eskiminizin. And, as a result, Cochise and his Chiricahuas were raiding from his mountain hide-out. And there were hostile bands of Coyoteros and Tontos roaming the hills and flatlands.

All because of Eskiminizin of the Aravaipa Apaches. The chief had asked military protection for himself and his half-starved people at Old Camp Grant. All he wanted was to again plant their fields in the valley of the Aravaipa, their homeland for generations. They were given permission by the Army to set up their wickiups. They were issued food and blankets, and it began to appear as though the first threads of peace were being woven at last between the Apache and the military.

But the barriers of greed and suspicion proved too strong. Word soon spread that Eskiminizin had bargained with the pony soldiers to the detriment of white settlers. Certain whites in the territory held to the frontier theory that there was no distinction between an Apache on the warpath and one content to live in peace; the only good Apaches were the dead ones.

Fuse to the powder keg was lighted when some Pinals conducted a raid on white settlers near San Xavier. During the skirmish a white man was killed. That was all the excuse needed.

An avenging party of whites, Mexicans, and Papago Indians were determined to exterminate Eskiminizin and his peaceful band as a warning to other Apaches.

It was after midnight when the raiders struck the village. Plans had been well-laid, catching the Aravaipas when asleep. Many of them managed to escape to the hills, but they left behind the bodies of 118 dead, eight of them men, the rest the mangled bodies of women and children clubbed to death in their sleep. Twenty-seven Apache children were taken prisoner and sold as slaves in Mexico. As a result of this treacherous attack upon a peaceful village, the whole territory was in turmoil.

Sundance pushed Eagle under the broiling sun, wanting to cover as much territory as possible. Although the map Grimholdt had drawn for him seemed fairly accurate, landmarks in that savage land of mountains and canyons slashed through lava and sand had a similarity about them.

But Sundance's ability to track even a moth in flight, as someone had once put it, stood him in good stead. He picked up Si Devlon's trail, and shortly past noon approached a high point of land shown on Grimholdt's map.

Devlon's mine, midway up a mountain, was well-protected. He had erected a four foot high rock wall at the rim of a narrow wedge of land overlooking the valley that could give him advance warning of approaching horsemen, provided they didn't sneak up on him through an almost impenetrable rock and brush filled ravine to the east. There were three mine tunnels in a steep cliff that rose abruptly beyond the rock wall; part of the cliff was an overhang that could be protection for Devlon should anyone try and come at him from above. The man would be reasonably safe if he didn't leave the protection of the overhang.

Sundance could see a black-whiskered man watching his approach. Sundance drew rein at the base of the promontory and shouted up some forty feet to the man above. He introduced himself and mentioned Grimholdt's name.

He was about to urge Eagle up a steep and twisting trail when a suspicious Devlon yelled a warning and pointed a .50 caliber Sharps rifle.

"Hold it right there, Sundance! Leave your hoss. An' your guns. Come up afoot, you want words."

Sundance said he'd reluctantly leave the horse and rifle. "But I'd sooner peel down to bare skin than be without my Colt."

Devlon debated, squinting down at him, then told him to come ahead. "But keep your hand away from that gun."

Sundance came up the steep zig-zag trail in long-legged strides, then reached the top. He saw a heavy plank gate that Devlon had not bothered to open. He vaulted over the stone wall.

Although Devlon was only a few years older than Sundance, he seemed awed. "I come up that trail afoot an' I'm puffin' an' snortin'. *You* come up that trail quicker'n a jack rabbit with a wind at his tail." Devlon wore a battered black hat, faded shirt with tobacco stains down the front, galluses, and dusty pants. He looked Sundance over out of light blue eyes. "When I first spotted you, I figured you was 'Pache. You ride like one. Then I seen that yaller hair."

A mesquite corral far along a slot between two cliffs held a burro and mule. Apparently Devlon lived in the larger of the tunnels. There was a stove and a tarp that could be lowered to keep out wind.

Sundance came right to the point, wanting to waste as little time as possible. "Grimholdt says you witnessed Burke Hunter's capture by Apaches."

Greed touched the bearded face. "Cost you twenty dollars."

Sundance would have paid twice that amount. He handed over a double eagle which Devlon dropped into his pocket. Devlon led the way over to a flat rock and told him to "set." Devlon sat on an upended keg. But he kept distance between himself and Sundance so that the Sharps was out of reach. That Devlon had survived in such hostile country proved him to be a man who took no unnecessary chances.

Devlon said he had first noticed Hunter prowling this country nearly a year ago. "Figured he was lookin' for somethin'. But didn't know where it was. I kept an eye on him."

"You began to trail him. To see if you could find out what he was up to?"

Devlon met Sundance's cool smile with one of his own. "Wa'al, last time I seen him he was pushin' a few head of hosses through the pass about nine, ten mile nawth." Devlon waved a calloused hand in that direction. "I knowed he was a hoss rancher so figured mebby he was short of money an' was headin' up to Fort Duncan to sell 'em to the cavalry."

"That when the Apaches grabbed him?"

"A dozen or so of them red devils . . . didn't do no shootin' though. Reckon they didn't want to chance hittin' the gal."

Sundance stiffened on the flat rock where he was sitting. To his left through the slot between cliffs he could see the flats stretching for miles to the east. Above towered the bluff that afforded a rock overhang to the tunnel entrances. He stared up at rock outcroppings on the cliff face, thinking he had seen something move. Then he decided it was the sun playing tricks. It had taken him that long to recover from the shock of Devlon's revelation.

"Hunter was traveling with a female that day?"

"Yep." Devlon smiled wolfishly through the black beard.

"He travel with her regularly?"

"First time I ever seen him with a woman in these here mountains. By the time I got field glasses on her, she had her back turned an' they was leadin' her away. She was settin' a saddle. Hunter was ridin' bareback."

Sundance stared thoughtfully at the miner. No white man would come into rough country without a saddle. Only an Indian felt comfortable riding bareback any distance. It might mean that Hunter had been unprepared for such an adventure as meeting up with a girl, turned his saddle over to her, and rode one of the loose horses with a hackamore.

"Living up here so long, you know Apaches,"

Sundance said. "Which bunch has got Hunter and the girl?"

Devlon failed to meet Sundance's eyes. "Don't rightly know. Might be one of them who busted away from ol' Mangus Colorado." Devlon spat, regarded the spittle balled at his feet in the gravel. Where they were sitting in the open, a cooling breeze tempered the afternoon heat. "Reckon you got your twenty dollars worth, Mr. Sundance. But on the other hand, I might recollect a little more. I tell you this much. Hunter's either dead or wishin' to Christ he was. Face up to it, Sundance. Them 'Paches stole some hosses. That alone is enough to bring the cavalry on their tails." Devlon paused for effect. "On top of that they kidnapped a purty gal."

"Grimholdt didn't say anything about you mentioning a girl in connection with Hunter."

"Never told nobody but you. Tell you this much," Devlon drawled. "If Hunter is wishin' he was dead, that gal by now is prayin' for it ten times over."

"There have been white women," Sundance said stiffly, "who never wanted to leave the Indian life."

"Heard them stories, sure, but never believed 'em. Was kinda s'prised Hunter's gal didn't grab his pistol an' put a bullet in her own head."

"How old do you think she was?"

"Young. The kind that'd make a man sweat in his dreams, what I could see of her."

"Seems Eloise Hunter has a rival she hasn't even heard of," Sundance said. "Tell me who's got Hunter and the girl?"

Devlon thrust out his bearded jaw. "I hear that every job you take is for big money. Wouldn't hurt to share it, huh?"

"I'll give you five dollars."

"Ten."

Sundance agreed, knowing he had had to let Devlon believe he got the best in the bargaining.

He started to dig into his pocket for another coin. A faint rattle of gravel came from above. Set in motion by an animal? Or a human. He thought he had seen movement before. This time he was not mistaken. He glimpsed a wedge of taut face peering around a rock outcropping midway up the sloping bluff. He had halfway expected the face to be Apache. This one belonged to a white man who had worked his way down the treacherous slope to take up position behind the jutting rock. The man, apparently unaware that he had been seen, showed a little more of himself in his sweated fawn-colored sombrero and dirty white shirt. He held a rifle and was gesturing with it to someone else out of sight higher up.

Then came Eagle's trumpeting, which meant that others were below. This was followed by a voice somehow familiar, coming from the foot of the promontory where Sundance had started his climb up the forty foot path.

"Hey, Sundance, you an' Devlon throw down your guns! Come to the wall where we can see you."

It was Hatch's voice. Devlon froze on his keg, the face whitening under the beard. "Son of a bitch," he breathed. "We set here talkin' an' I let somebody sneak up."

The man from above was standing now, pointing the rifle. "You're covered from up here! You with the yaller hair! Throw down your gun! Quick! Or that bastard next to you will have the back of his head blowed off!"

It had taken no more than a dozen heartbeats

since Sundance had glimpsed the man above. Devlon, cradling the Sharps, his back to the rifleman above, stared in awe at the speed with which Sundance leaped to his feet and drew the Colt. Sundance fired at the man on the bluff. It was a poor target because the man ducked behind the outcropping. Then Sundance crashed into Devlon, knocking him off the keg and under the shelter of the overhang.

5

Devlon landed on hands and knees, but retained his grip on the Sharps. Rifle fire from above raked the keg where he had been sitting not a moment before.

"Cover the one below, that goddamned Hatch!" Sundance yelled. "But be careful of my horse!"

Sundance sprang from the shelter of the overhang to seek out the pale taut face that had first alerted him to danger. So far as he knew, there were two men above. Sundance saw the fawn-colored hat move and saw the face again. He fired twice. The face collapsed. A dropped rifle began sliding down the face of the bluff, raising dust. An instant later its owner, who had clung to the protective rock ledge, lost his grip on this also. He cartwheeled in midair before landing with a thump of crushed bone and cartilage against the hardpan.

Devlon was at the rock wall, shouting over his shoulder. "Fella below has got a white shirt he's wavin' as a flag of truce!"

"All we wanted to do was talk!" Hatch yelled up. "And Charlie had to go and jump the gun on me!"

"Talk about what?" Devlon yelled down at him.

"Gold! Sundance got it out of the Hunter woman, I'll bet on it! We trailed him here and . . . Oh, hell, there's more'n enough for all of us."

Sundance did not dare move, because it would mean turning his back on the second attacker above that he still hadn't seen. "Keep down, Devlon!" he warned. "Don't listen to Hatch! It's a trick of some kind, sure as hell."

Devlon grinned over his shoulder at Sundance. "Then there *is* somethin' to that business about Hunter's gold . . ."

"Damn it, Devlon, keep your eye on Hatch!" Sundance warned again, his gaze sweeping the face of the boulder-strewn cliff overhead.

"But he's got that flag of truce, so mebby we oughta hear what he's gotta say . . ."

But Sundance could waste no more breath trying to explain why you couldn't trust a man, flag of truce or not, who was low enough to torture information out of a woman by branding her with a red hot spike.

Not one man above, but two. A rifle shot smashed down from the lip of the bluff; Sundance felt a twitching of buckskin shirt along his left side. All he could see above now was an oily smudge of powdersmoke. Then a man in a striped shirt with a rifle. Sundance fired three times, and heard a scream of pain. More gravel cascaded. The man in the striped shirt leaned over the lip of the bluff and tumbled some twenty feet to crash head first into the ledge of rock that had sheltered his companion now crumpled on the hardpan. From the corner of his eye, Sundance caught sight of the third man above, trying to reach a spire of rock. Sundance fired, but the bullet whipped harmlessly into the pale blue sky.

He whirled in time to see a rangy, scarfaced man to Devlon's left, beyond the gate in the rock wall. He was a man who no doubt had come up through the brush from the ravine that abutted the promontory base to the east, and had not used the path where Hatch in plain sight with the flag of truce acted as decoy. The scarfaced man wearing a concha-banded hat panted from the fast climb. But he grinned as he started to lift a rifle on the unsuspecting Devlon. Sundance yelled a warning, but Devlon's instinct caused him to spin around. Devlon's Sharps spoke before the rifle. Sundance saw the lower half of the stranger's face sheared off by the .50 caliber bolt of lead.

"Devlon, get back!" Sundance shouted, because the man was in a direct line of the rifleman above; Devlon, in his eagerness to get a shot at the treacherous Hatch and the flag of truce, was leaning over the rock wall.

"Nothin' like a whiff of gold dust to bring the snakes outta their holes!" Devlon gave a snort of laughter. "Reckon me helpin' you fight off these bastards earns me a share . . ."

But an enraged voice from above yelled, "You just killed my *brother*!" He shot Devlon in the back but did not kill him.

The man, wearing leather chaps and bandoleers, danced along the lip of the bluff, firing down at Sundance. One of the bullets, ricocheting off the boot heel of the first dead attacker, sprawled in the slot where Sundance crouched. And before the man above could adjust his aim to make a kill, Sundance shot him twice in the midriff. He fell off the bluff, screaming, and crashed into the brushy ravine below.

And then came a pounding of hooves, receding rapidly. Sundance rushed to the wall. His heart froze when he saw no sign of Eagle for a minute, then saw him out on the flats. Hatch or the other one might have made a grab for him, and Eagle pulled away.

It was the red-mustached Hatch making his escape through the ravine, no doubt about it. At the foot of the promontory was the white shirt he had used as a flag of truce. Talk of gold had made Devlon careless.

Sundance held his fire when he had a distant glimpse of Hatch bent over the neck of a galloping pinto. It was no time to waste more ammunition that later on might save his life. Twice, Hatch had made good his escape only because Sundance was without his Henry rifle with the greater range than the Colt.

Next time, Sundance vowed. It would be foolish to go after him. By the time he raced down the trail and boarded Eagle, Hatch would have a lead that might take hours to close.

More important was Devlon. The man had a bad wound in the back, quite possibly fatal. And when Sundance carried him to blankets inside the mine tunnel, he was sure of it.

He knelt beside Devlon. "Tell me what you know. I'll pay double, even triple what you ask." Mention of a price was only a gesture; the miner had only a few more minutes of life. His face was graying, the eyes growing dull. Sundance leaned close so as not to miss a word. "Where are the Apaches holding Hunter? I'm damn sure you know. I'll find it but you'll save me time if you tell . . ."

"El Tigre . . ." Devlon gasped.

"Means tiger in Spanish."

"Chief... Apache chief he is..." He smiled weakly. "Figured to... to string you along. Get more money..."

"Tell me about El Tigre, Devlon."

"Apache name is Sana... calls hisself El Tigre now..."

And when the voice trailed away, Sundance said urgently, "Where's his hideout?"

Devlon's lips twitched as if trying desperately to stem his fading strength and speak. "Big Luke... he guide you..."

Mention of the half-breed Navajo, former scout condemned to Army gallows for murder, caused Sundance to stiffen. "What makes you think he's going to guide me..."

"Big as any grizzly, damn if he ain't, an' twice as mean." He grinned up at Sundance through the beard. "Man could lose his hair if he got careless around that big bastard."

"Devlon, don't waste strength or words. I want El Tigre. You must know..."

Devlon said, "Nawth." He gestured in that direction. Life ran out of him.

Sundance swore in frustration. At the wall he scanned the miles of flatlands. He saw dust far to the south. Hatch?

He did take time to dismantle part of the rock wall and used the rocks for a cairn. At least it would keep predators from Devlon's body. Predators were welcome to the others.

Hours later, traversing a long canyon, he noticed a moving cloud of dust some miles to the east. Because of rocks lining the canyon rim, he could not see what was causing it. He loosened the Henry rifle in its boot, speculating on who the rider or riders might be. A breeze had come up so that the dust was smudged into a cloud, making it difficult to tell whether it was one rider or ten. Who was stalking him? White man? Red? Or was the dust simply from wild animals on the move? In any event it was no time for mistakes. And to further complicate the deadly game Sundance had contracted to play, was the female prisoner. If Si Devlon could be believed, that is.

Devlon, one of those unknowns who roamed dangerous country looking for riches. Rarely did they make a strike as Burke Hunter seemed to have done. Most barely eked out an existence. A man made better wages clerking in a store, riches compared to what most prospectors found in a lifetime. But you couldn't convince them because they had their dreams. After all, Sundance wondered, was there much more for these men than dreams?

Sundance's thoughts had been wandering in the heat haze as he pushed north. It was no time for a mental lapse. With the territory aflame with hatred and suspicion, Sundance knew he could afford to lose little time in making the transition from white man to Cheyenne Dog Soldier. Until this could be accomplished he was more vulnerable than most, his long yellow hair an inviting target for any roaming bands of Chiricahuas or Tontos.

For an hour or more there had been no sign of the moving balloon of dust that had paralleled his progress through the canyon. But he did not let down his guard.

With the last of day a bright band on the horizon, he spotted greenery midway up a wide and brushy cul-de-sac. It meant water. Water attracted predators, not only four legged, but two.

Leaving Eagle near a screen of mesquite and tall rocks, he approached on foot, cradling the Henry rifle, eyes straining against shadows thrown by black cottonwoods around a spring. But he saw no sign of movement. A faint stream of water bubbled from the ground and flowed downslope where it finally disappeared in deep sand. His trained eye studied signs, tracks of wild animals, and of horses, shod and unshod. It was a watering place visited by Indian and white, but not recently, and the horse tracks were at least a week old.

He brought Eagle to the springs, unlashed the bags of buffalo hide, then unsaddled. After the horse had his fill of water, Sundance turned him loose on a grassy plot some twenty yards upslope, beyond the cottonwoods. He needed food and it was unwise to hunt with a rifle. He unlaced bindings of one of the bags and was just reaching for bow and arrow when a sound alerted him, a rustling so slight it would have been unnoticed by most men. Standing utterly still, he waited, then was rewarded by movement near the top of the cul-de-sac, a glimpse of an animal through some box elders.

Soundlessly he reached deep into the long cylindrical bag and drew out a perfectly balanced throwing ax, a tomahawk, as white men called the lethal weapon.

Motionless in the shadows, Sundance watched a burro deer move nimble-footed down the slope, nose in the air, nostrils twitching. Obviously it had caught Eagle's scent upslope, but not that of man. Sundance waited patiently, and crouched downwind from the cautious animal now nearing the springs. His fingers tightened around the short hickory handle of the throwing ax as the deer started to bury its nose in the water. Sundance made an overhand movement, hurling the ax with such accuracy that its blade cleaved the skull. Without a sound, the deer dropped.

Sundance sprang forward, retrieved his ax, cleansed the blade, then used his Bowie knife that had been fashioned for him by the same artisan who had produced the balanced throwing ax. Quickly he butchered the deer, saving enough of the choice cuts for another meal. He dragged the remains deep into the brush, then built a small fire. It had been a long day for both himself and his horse. There had been one bit of luck that Hatch, in his rage and frustration, hadn't shot the big horse dead there at the foot of the promontory before getting away.

As shadows deepened, he considered his chances of securing Burke Hunter's release from El Tigre and earning the money called for by his contract with Eloise Hunter. Money that Sundance needed desperately. A stirring of the leaves told him that more of those in high command in the Army were growing sick of the savagery directed against the Indian, the disgust intensified since the massacre of the Aravaipa women and children. At long last there seemed to be a real chance for a peace between white man and Indian. But the one language those politicos in Washington with sufficient power to agree to was the language of gold.

Even without the lure of gold, there was the crippled Eddie Strong to be avenged. Before it was over, Sundance intended to repay Burke Hunter in kind for the butchery.

Sundance knew there should be no further delay

in making his transition to Cheyenne Dog Soldier. His chances of survival would be slim enough as a blood brother in a hostile Apache camp, but he'd have none at all if he entered their domain as a white. He spoke their language. It would not be easy. But what in these last years had been easy?

In pulling off his buckskin shirt, he noticed for the first time a fresh bullet hole near the left armpit. A few inches more, and it would have taken his heart instead of merely puncturing his buckskin. He shrugged off the near-miss, as he had so many others in the past. After stripping off his clothing, he washed off trail dust in the springs, then bound his loins and stepped again into his moccasins. His torso, with its numerous scars, glistened from the creek water; scars made by bullet, arrow, war-lance, and those more prominent, which came from his initiation into the elite of Cheyenne warriors, the Dog Soldiers.

While the venison sizzled and sputtered on the coals, he unlashed his bedroll. Deep in the blankets was one of his greatest treasures, a Cheyenne war bonnet of beadwork and eagle feathers, the head-band decorated with conchas and tails of ermine, a symbol of what he had achieved as a young Cheyenne. Reverently he shook out the war bonnet so that the painted feathers rustled softly in the thickening twilight. Few among the Cheyennes had been able to earn a war bonnet by the age of twenty.

He put aside his war bonnet and inspected his short-curved bow of juniper, tipped with buffalo horn. He twanged the bowstring made from a sinew from the shoulder tendon of a tough bull buffalo. A bow such as this was the first weapon he had mastered as a boy. But this one was even more powerful, capable of whipping an arrow four hundred yards on target. At closer range it could drive an arrow shaft clear through a buffalo at a dead run, and if necessary, through the body of a man.

From a quiver of panther skin, the tail still attached, he withdrew his arrows, one by one. Each shaft he had painstakingly perfected on his own straightening stone. Each was feathered with buzzard quills, the arrow heads of chipped flint. Then he looked over the throwing ax. Knowing its blade had been dulled slightly from crashing into the skull of the burro deer, he sharpened its edge on a small whetstone. Finally he tested the blade with his thumb and was satisfied it was razor sharp as the big Bowie knife.

This inspection of weapons was a ritual done whenever from choice or necessity he made the transition from white man to red. There could be no flaw. And each arrow had to be true. If any of the feathered tips were disarranged it could throw off the aim. And in the hazardous life he had chosen to lead, not even a minor error could be tolerated.

Especially in the job he had agreed to undertake for Eloise Hunter. From the moment he entered the Apache camp to try and effect Burke Hunter's release, he could be fighting for his life with the Indian weapons. Long practice had made him a master of each. He looked over his war lance, was satisfied, and put it and the other weapons aside. It was time to relax, to ease tensions created from having had to fight against odds at the Hunter ranch. And today at the Devlon mine.

Some men relaxed with whiskey in camp. Not Sundance. It was something learned after the greatest tragedy of his life some years ago. Since then, when consuming more than two stiff drinks at any one time, he risked changing from a self-possessed professional fighter into a kind of madman not responsible for his actions. Too much of the frontier whiskey could unlock secret horrors from the past and send him on a rampage. He never carried a bottle with him for this reason and bought whiskey only one drink at a time.

Instead of camp whiskey, he found relaxation in the marijuana smoked in his pipe. This he preferred to the customary Cheyenne mixture of tobacco and red willow bark. Some Indians used peyote in the ritual of escaping from the trials of life. He preferred this weed.

After lighting the contents of the clay bowl with a coal, he drew on it, then lifted his pipe in ritual to the darkening sky, then to the four points of the compass. Only when this solemn rite was completed did he draw deeply, savoring the smoke. Tensions began to uncoil in his long body.

Finally he put aside the pipe and used the broad blade of the Bowie knife to slice into the roasted venison. As he ate his supper he gave an appearance of being at ease. But he was always alert, every nerve attuned to instantly evaluate any foreign sound or sudden flight of birds. A rodent abruptly scampering with lifted tail toward the sanctuary of its hole could tell a story of potential danger, but mainly he listened for sounds from Eagle, or watched his shadowy figure upslope through the black cottonwoods. Peacefully chomping grass meant that all was well. But a suddenly lifted head or a whinny could mean trouble. Sundance ate more of the venison, carefully wiping grease from fingertips on grass near his thigh.

With his belly filled, he treated himself to one final luxury. He unlaced the round bag always lashed to Eagle's saddle, which held the symbol of his valor as a Cheyenne: his shield. It was slightly less than three feet in diameter, fashioned from the tough neck hide of a bull buffalo, dried and then shrunken over a circle of juniper wood. Next to the hide was a layer of dried gramma grass; over this, deer skin had been stretched, taut as a war drum. On this had been painted a Thunderbird, the most sacred of medicines to a Cheyenne Dog Soldier. It was his warrior's luck as well as protection in combat because it could stop an arrow, divert a war lance, and even blunt the force of a musket ball. Even though it was of little use against the powerful rifles now coming into use across the frontier, he would always have it within reach.

Gazing at it reverently, he held it at arm's length. Then his lips thinned. In the faint haze of smoke drifting from his cook fire could be seen six scalps dangling from the lower edge of the shield. The only scalps he had ever taken. Three of them were coarse, midnight black, the scalplocks of Indians. Hair of the other three was shorter, one brown, one reddish, and the third a shade darker yellow than his own.

On the tragic day he had vowed to take those six scalps his life had changed from that of Cheyenne warrior to avenger.

6

That night Sundance slept little; he sensed an alien presence but could see nor hear anything suspicious. Eagle seemed restive. Sundance would nap for a time, his back to a tree trunk, then he would scout the area and pick another spot to catch a little sleep. At hand this night were weapons of both Indian and white. If outnumbered, he would use the Henry rifle and Colt. But if there was only one attacker or even two, then the bow with its whirring message of death would end the threat silently, and there would be no gunshot to warn other potential enemies who might be nearby.

After a breakfast of venison, Sundance was about to put away his Thunderbird shield when Eagle, grazing steadily on grass upslope, grew suddenly quiet.

Sundance dropped his Thunderbird shield and picked up his bow. In the uncertain light of predawn he noiselessly slipped into the shadows of black cottonwoods, unmoving as if part of the trees. In a few moments he saw a huge man striding up the grade. He wore a headband and tunic, leggings and moccasins.

Sundance stepped in view, his bow lifted. "Far enough; or you'll have no throat." He spoke in Cheyenne.

"I come to talk, not to shoot."

Sundance's reply to that was cold laughter. "You're Big Luke?"

"I am part Navajo and understand your language. I spent time on the high plains as a boy."

"Where's your horse?"

"Back there." Luke gestured over his shoulder. "If I rode a horse, you would hear it. And you might shoot. I came silently on foot to get close enough so that you'd see I was a blood brother."

"Or close enough to cut my throat while I slept?" Sundance's lips thinned. "Hold your hands out in front where I can see them. Then come sit by my blanket."

"You are a suspicious Cheyenne."

"One reason I've been able to live this long."

Big Luke drew closer, hands in front as Sundance had ordered. He sank to the ground. Although he weighed some two hundred and fifty pounds, he moved gracefully. "I saw you once at Bent's Fort," Luke said. "You were younger then. But so was I." He laughed. His teeth were large in proportion to the cavernous mouth. His only weapon seemed to be a pistol in a cross-draw holster.

Memory of Bent's Fort sent a chill through Sundance. But he wasn't going to allow himself to be tricked; perhaps Luke remembered him from those days. Maybe he had only heard about them from others.

Seen up close in the suddenly growing daylight, the ex-scout's face bore deep scars at cheekbones and eye corners, and scar tissue on the knuckles of broad-fisted hands.

"I remember your parents at Bent's Fort," Big Luke said. "Your father, the Englishman. And your Cheyenne mother, the chief's daughter."

"Who's waiting for you back in the brush?" Sundance demanded, seaching the downslope with his narrowed eyes.

"I travel alone."

Sundance's lips curled. He mentioned the dust cloud that had paralleled his ride through the canyon yesterday. "One rider or more. You and your bunch?"

Luke switched to English. "Mebby it was the white man, the only hombre you didn't kill at Devlon's mine."

"So you were in with them!" Sundance accused.

"I heard shooting. By the time I got there it was over. I saw the dead. You were gone."

Sundance's bark of laughter was an unpleasant sound. Again he flicked his gaze down the rocky terrain that stretched away to the flats. He saw no movement. Putting his scornful gaze back on the big man, he said, "The name Hatch mean anything to you?"

"Heard of him."

"You're in it with him. You let him risk his neck while you hung back."

Luke shook his massive head. "No. But I was close enough to see the live one run away."

"That was Hatch." Sundance regarded him coldly. "What the hell were you doing that close to Devlon's mine?"

"Grimholdt said that's where you had gone."

Sundance felt disappointed in the assayer. "Grimholdt talked?"

"He didn't want to." Black eyes danced. "But there are ways."

"Damn it, you killed him!"

Big Luke threw up an arm in defense as Sundance's fingers tightened on the nocked arrow. "Wait!" he shouted. "I didn't even cut him. Had to twist his fingers a little. Then I knocked him out. He'll be all right."

"If he isn't, I'll come looking for you."

Big Luke reached out to touch the Thunderbird shield Sundance had not yet stowed away in its round carrying bag. Luke fingered the scalps affixed to it. "So you take hair," he said laughing. "I never bother."

"Only those six did I ever take," Sundance said in a tight voice.

"Something to do with your parents," Luke said, speaking in Cheyenne, "so I once heard."

"I don't talk about it. What I will talk about is Burke Hunter."

"Put down the bow, my brother. I am here as a friend."

"My arrow aimed at your throat insures that friendship."

Big Luke held out his long brown fingers so that Sundance could see the scarred knuckles. "I could tear you apart with these hands."

"You won't get the chance."

Big Luke laughed. "You better pray that I won't."

"Tell me about El Tigre. That's no Apache name. Any more than Big Luke is Navajo."

"El Tigre's Apache name is Sana. My Navajo name is Fire Tree. I prefer Big Luke."

Sundance wanted to keep him talking to learn as

much as possible before making a decision. He asked about the letter smuggled out of camp from Hunter to his wife. "Who delivered the letter?"

"My friend Black Moccasin. I have other friends."

"Is Hunter still alive?"

"I've seen him three times at camp."

"Why does El Tigre let you come and go at will? You're not Apache."

Big Luke bared his teeth. "Because he knows how I hate the pony soldiers. Even worse than he does. I once scouted for them, the Army. They paid me back by sentencing me to die on their gallows. I escaped."

"You murdered a pony soldier?"

"A Yuma scout. He deserved more than the quick death he got from me. He stole my woman." Big Luke's eyes were fierce. "Now I want another woman. I ache with the wanting the three times I see her. I look on her and my heart soars."

"Poetic you are in the Cheyenne tongue," Sundance said thinly. "You mean the captive white woman?"

"Lila Corey is her name. I want sons by her. A mix of blood is good. Like mine and yours. My mother was Navajo, my father one of the mountain men."

Mention of mountain men caused Sundance to stiffen, head back, lips suddenly pale. But not a tremor in the hands that gripped bow and arrow.

Big Luke was surprised at Sundance's reaction. "You show hatred. For which? Navajo or mountain men?"

"There's good in both, I admit." Sundance exhaled a tight breath, angered at himself for showing his feelings concerning tragic events some years before near Bent's Fort. He forced his mind back to the present, masking out the old horror. He asked why El Tigre had kept Burke Hunter alive all these weeks.

"Only because he's managed to kill the best knife fighters among the Apaches," was Luke's smiling reply.

"Hunter the knife expert," Sundance muttered coldly.

"I am afraid of no one," Big Luke said, still speaking Cheyenne, "yet I would not want to face him with cold steel." Luke paused and looked at Sundance speculatively. "They say you are also an expert with your Bowie knife."

Sundance discounted the flattery. "You can guide me to El Tigre's hideout."

"We must plan carefully. I go tell El Tigre that you fight Burke Hunter with a knife. El Tigre does not like Hunter. But he also thinks he has some kind of spirit power. His medicine tells him it is so."

"And the rest of your plan, Big Luke?"

"You beat Hunter in the fight," Luke said, then added sharply, "but don't kill him. We want him alive to take him with us. To tell us what he knows." Big Luke the conspirator winked broadly.

"Why would El Tigre let him go with us? Or even let us go, for that matter?"

"El Tigre will say you are good medicine, because you whipped Hunter, who had stood up to three of the best knife fighters in the tribe. El Tigre will give you anything you want."

Sundance gave a faint nod, sensing what the big man was leading up to. "And what *will* I want?"

"Hunter. And the girl." Luke's eyes brightened. "He'll give you Hunter because you defeated him."

"Why will he give me the girl?"

"You will say you want her as your woman. She

will be your prize." And when Sundance just looked at him, Luke frowned and said, "He will make you these two presents, Hunter and the girl. I will talk to Many Wolves to make sure. He is the medicine man."

"The medicine man will listen to you, Big Luke?"

Luke grinned. "El Tigre listens to Many Wolves. That is more important." He shrugged one of his massive shoulders. "Yes, we can do this, the two of us."

"You make it sound easy."

"Your fight with Hunter will not be easy. But once you have whipped him . . ." Luke leaned forward. "We have two days, maybe three. There are only a few braves in camp. El Tigre sent most of his men south. To steal horses. I told him where he could find a thousand head of good horses."

Sundance studied the broad face with its numerous scars. "Why didn't El Tigre go with his men on the horse raid?" he asked narrowly.

"He is too busy with his medicine man. He believes strongly in such foolishness. I don't."

"It isn't always foolishness."

"Many Wolves . . . older than the moon and with the mind of a child. But El Tigre swears he speaks with someone from the land of shadows. It is all we need." Luke grinned. "You agree that with most of the men gone from camp, with me whispering in the ear of that old fool Many Wolves, we can do it?"

Sundance, sniffing double cross, said, "And if we get out of El Tigre's camp . . . *if* we do. Then what?"

"Simple. I want half of the gold. And the girl."

"What if she doesn't agree?"

Big Luke showed his teeth. "Tame a woman like you tame a horse."

"What will El Tigre say to all this?"

"He'll give you Hunter and the girl," Luke said impatiently. "And the bag of nuggets Hunter had with him when he was captured. Then we'll make Hunter tell us where the mine is."

"Why doesn't El Tigre get it out of him?"

Big Luke gave a snort of laughter. "Because he already knows where it is."

"Then you're talking about Apache gold?" Sundance said softly. "Their sacred gold?"

"Nothing's sacred," Big Luke said, his voice turning ugly, "but money. And a woman that catches your eye. Lila Corey."

"The girl makes her own choice."

Luke stared. "What'd you say?" he demanded, switching to English.

"I'll bargain gold, but never a woman."

"I want her even more than gold," Luke said, the words hissing through the large teeth. "I'll *have* her, by God!" He levered himself to his feet, casting a huge shadow across the sand. He turned his back as if to stride away. Then he spun around, his right hand reaching for the pistol in the cross-draw holster. Sundance wasn't fooled. Big Luke froze when he saw Sundance pull back on the drawstring of his bow, saw the arrow poised for lethal flight. Luke lowered his hand.

"You back off, Sundance. Mebby you don't know it, but your job is to do what I say."

"You make another move for that gun, and you're dead."

"I'm the same as a colonel here. You see I remember how it is in the Army. You're just a plain trooper. You take orders."

"I obey no man." Sundance's lips curled. "Much

less the likes of you. Murdered a blood brother, a Yuma scout. In a fight over a woman."

"You try to do this job by yourself an' I'll get El Tigre's ear. I'll let him know you're bad medicine—a half-breed Cheyenne who sometimes hunts down his own kind."

"I hunt down those who deserve it. Happens that some of them are Indian."

"I offer you a chance and you spit in my face!" Luke was roaring now, his voice filling the cul-de-sac, reaching out to the rock-filled, brushy flats below. "Know how El Tigre treats his enemies? He'll smear your body with honey. Then stake you over an ant hill. When the wind is right, they'll be able to hear your screams clear to Sonora."

"Never mind shouting. So your friends can hear you and come at a run." Sundance's voice hardened. "Tell 'em to keep their distance, or you'll have this arrow in your guts!"

"What friends?"

"The ones riding with you yesterday. Who helped kick up dust at the rim of the canyon. *Tell 'em to stay back*!"

Fury rode the wide face and Sundance knew he had guessed right. Luke looked apprehensively at the arrow pointed at his stomach. Turning his head slightly he shouted an order in Apache.

"Turn your back, Luke," Sundance ordered. "I mean it."

Luke hesitated, then obeyed. And in that moment, Sundance dropped his bow and arrow and scooped up the Colt, drawing back the hammer with his thumb.

"Now it doesn't make a damn bit of difference whether anybody hears a gunshot or not. If your friends try and ride in, they'll be dead along with you. Face me so I can watch your hands. Lift your gun...carefully. Put it on the ground. Then step back."

Luke reddened in rage and humiliation. When the gun was on the ground, Sundance waved him aside and kicked the weapon, which clattered into some rocks twenty yards away.

Sundance added further humiliation by forcing him to lie face down on the ground while he quickly broke camp. But he kept one eye on the unarmed and fuming Army scout. After Eagle was ready for the trail, Sundance dropped the loop of a catch rope over Big Luke's neck and forced him to walk downslope a few feet ahead of Eagle. Sundance rode behind him, Henry rifle balanced across his thigh.

"You're taking me to El Tigre's camp," Sundance said. "On my terms."

"Over my dead body," Big Luke shouted back.

"If that's the way it has to be," Sundance said calmly.

Big Luke cursed as they moved slowly in the morning light down out of the cul-de-sac with its cottonwoods and springs. They reached lower levels where the land smoothed out for endless miles, dotted occasionally by immense shafts of rock. Here giant sahuaros threw grotesque shadows.

"How many men with you?" Sundance demanded. He rode close, the muzzle of the cocked rifle inches from the enraged Luke. Only a slight pressure of the trigger would blow off his head.

"Go to hell!" Luke thundered.

Sundance jerked back on the rope. Luke made strangling sounds and caught at the noose with both hands.

Sundance repeated his question.

There were three, Luke finally admitted, fighting his anger. And to prove their toughness he said they had formerly been with the great Apache chief Cochise. "Now they're with *me*!"

Sundance knew what it meant; Indians breaking away from their own chief, for one reason or another, to follow a condemned murderer like Big Luke. Not at all uncommon on the frontier. It was such men banding together who accounted for much of the savagery.

Luke faced him, the black eyes with scars at the corners bright with fury. "You've signed your death warrant, Sundance!"

"My death warrant has been signed many times. It'll be signed many times in the future." They had halted in a clearing, their dust filtering through the deep green of mesquite. The sun was a red ball in the east, shooting colors into the horizon.

"What now, Cheyenne?" Luke sneered.

"Tell one of your friends to bring up your horse. We can cover ground faster that way. But it's up to you. You can walk all the way to El Tigre's camp. Won't matter to me."

As he talked, Sundance's eyes swept the clumps of rocks, the brush, looking for any sign of movement. Luke's men were well-hidden.

Luke shouted, "Black Moccasin! My horse!"

Black Moccasin obeyed the shouted order in Apache. He appeared, leading a roan saddler. He had the broad Apache face, the glittering black eyes. His headband was of faded red cloth.

Big Luke, trembling with rage, ordered the scowling Black Moccasin to get back with the other two.

"Don't try and follow us!" Sundance shouted at the broad-shouldered Apache. "Get within half a mile and I'll shoot Luke in the back!"

Black Moccasin understood the threat in Apache. He looked back at Big Luke standing there in the warming sun with a noose around his neck. It would take some effort, Sundance knew, for Big Luke to erase the memory of this scene from the minds of his three followers.

Sundance waited until Black Moccasin was riding east at a lope, soon joined by two more Apaches, before ordering Luke into the saddle. He had already made sure there were no weapons in the roan's saddlebags.

"Remember this," Sundance warned the sullen Luke, "if anybody gives me trouble, your brains'll be on the ground."

"You're the biggest damn fool in history, Cheyenne," Luke snarled. "To turn against me only because I want a certain woman for my own!"

"You didn't fool me. Even if I'd agree to go along with your plan, you'd have double-crossed me in the end."

"Now you're headin' into an even bigger trap!"

"Get going. El Tigre's camp. I'd waste time trying to find it on my own. So that's why you're going to oblige."

"What if I say try and *make* me do it?" Luke threatened.

Sundance only smiled. Big Luke got its meaning. He started riding west and north toward a wall of mountains rimmed with cloud banks.

7

It was two hours of steady riding before Big Luke reined in his roan and faced Sundance. The look of sincerity on the broad, scarred face was laughable.

"We're blood brothers," Luke said in Apache. "It is with sorrow that I remember some of the things I said. As I told you, you need me. We go to El Tigre's camp together, eh?"

"I go alone." Sundance one-handedly pointed the Henry rifle at the broad chest. Luke swore, the look of contrition in the black eyes replaced by cold fury.

El Tigre's lair was located high among pinnacle rocks, the approach reached by an obscure trail. Surrounding it was a tumbled country of bleak hills, a maze of canyons. As they neared the towering, flat-topped mountain, rimmed by high rocks, Sundance saw two minute figures appear on a high ledge. After another quarter of a mile he could tell that they were two stocky Apaches wearing bandoleers, black hair held in place by headbands of red. Both held rifles as they peered down.

Sundance ordered Big Luke to halt, then lifted his right hand in the sign of peace. He shouted up at the two sentinels in the Apache he had picked up some years ago while mingling with the tribes.

"I am Sundance, of the Cheyennes!" But whether they could hear him or not because of the distance, he didn't know. One of them left the ledge.

Sundance turned to Luke and said tensely, "I go the rest of the way alone."

Luke frowned. "Now that we've come this far, you better take me with you," he said in English. "I know El Tigre, you don't."

"So you can tell your lies about me. As you already threatened."

Luke made one final attempt. "Remember this, Sundance. I could hate you for the way you made a fool of me in front of my friends. But I can forget all that if we be partners, eh?" The smile strained. "Like I wanted from the first. We both got mad and said things."

"Go back the way we came." Sundance jerked his head to the east, keeping one eye on the ledge above.

Luke continued, the last of his self-control slipping away. "I tell you this, Cheyenne. You touch that girl, an' you'll pray for death on an ant hill. 'Cause the one you get from me will be a thousand times worse."

"Get out of here, Luke! I won't tell you again!"

Sundance saw that the sentry had rejoined his companion on the ledge. When Luke opened his mouth as if to shout up at them, Sundance gave him a final warning. "Not one word, Luke. Not one word. Killing you would be a pleasure."

Big Luke looked at him and then at the Henry

rifle. He jerked the roan's head around brutally and pounded away, raising a plume of yellow dust.

A third Apache appeared on the ledge, obviously summoned by the one who had slipped away and then returned. This one stared down at Sundance, who was astride Eagle at the foot of the steep mountain. This man stood with arms folded in the manner of a chief. The chief stalked away. Then the two sentries beckoned to Sundance. The trail was steep, tortuous, but at last he reached a clearing between towering rocks. It was over a half mile long, a quarter of that in width. His trained eye estimated a hundred or more wickiups of the traditional reed and brush. Some twenty braves were lined up facing him, a few armed with rifles, the rest with bow and war lance. The man of the ledge stood in their center, jaw outthrust, arms folded. He was in his fifties, the face lined, but there was little gray in the hair that reached the shoulders. He wore tunic, leggings, and moccasins. His eyes were fierce.

Sundance rode close and dismounted. "I am Sundance of the *Iss-io-me-tan-iu* band of the Cheyennes."

"Welcome to my camp. I know why you are here. Your coming was spoken from the land of shadows. You are here to fight to the death with a knife." The man looked him over, the moccasins, leggings, breech clout, the bared chest, the headband. "I am El Tigre, born as Sana and renamed for the fierce jaguar by the Mexicans I raided so often. I like the name. I kept it."

A stooped old man with long gray hair and watery eyes stepped from a wickiup. He was bent nearly double and used a cane to keep from toppling. He came to El Tigre's side and the chief leaned down, showing great respect, and listened gravely to what the old man had to say.

El Tigre straightened up and said, "Many Wolves, this is the medicine you said would come," pointing at the impassive Sundance.

El Tigre said that Sundance could ride Eagle to the horse herd, unsaddle, and then return to him. Sundance, trailed by two mounted braves, rode slowly past curious squaws and younger Apache women. He hoped to see Lila Corey, but there was no sign of her, nor of the other white captive, Burke Hunter. What he did notice, however, was a maiden with sleek black hair, prettier than the rest, who stared at him openly and seemed on the verge of speaking. When a flicker of a smile touched his lips, she turned and walked away into the crowd of squaws. Many squaws, but few braves, he noticed. He recalled Luke mentioning that most of the braves were away on a horse raid. That much truth, apparently, spoken by the renegade.

Sundance endured the stares of the Apaches; this tall Cheyenne with scarred chest, riding a magnificent Nez Perce war horse.

Later, upon retracing his steps, this time on foot, he was subjected to even closer scrutiny. He looked for the Apache maiden but did not see her.

He was given food and water and then once again was facing the solidly built El Tigre. The chief spoke gravely. "You must be tired and you need rest before you fight Blood Knife to the death."

"Blood Knife?"

"The man known by whites as Burke Hunter. We have given him a new name because he is deadly with cold steel."

"Blood Knife. A name well chosen," Sundance

said with no shred of emotion showing on his face. But his heart was beating faster. Face to face with the bastard at last!

"Someone from the land of shadows sent us Blood Knife," El Tigre continued. "As you were sent. A prophecy made by Many Wolves."

"A great medicine man, I can see."

"Whichever one of you survives in combat will be rewarded," El Tigre said, "with gold. And with a virgin with hair the color of yours." He meant Lila Corey, Sundance was sure. And he knew Indians; El Tigre would not likely speak of virginity unless older squaws at his orders had made sure.

Sundance said, "You mentioned gold if I win against Blood Knife. How much?"

"Thirty of the nuggets Blood Knife had when he was sent to us."

Sundance waited, wondering if the chief might mention the mine Hunter had apparently found. El Tigre watched him a moment, the eyes reflecting faint amusement. "Gold interests you, not the woman? Another, a half-breed Navajo, wants her desperately."

"Big Luke. So you know about him."

"*All* about him." Sundance wondered just what that meant. El Tigre said, "We believe you and Blood Knife to be good medicine, as is this girl we now call Sunflower because of the color of her hair." The chief stood with arms folded, jaw outthrust, the voice now hardening. "Since the massacre of Eskiminizin's people, who were my friends, we have killed many whites. We will kill more. The other chiefs hold back in their vengeance. So I am acting alone. It is I who am destined to lead my people in driving out the pony soldiers and then the whites."

This he said in English, which Sundance guessed was understood by few of the Apaches, if any.

Then El Tigre said, "You seem surprised, Sundance, that I speak the white language. When I was a boy, I was taken to Mexico, raised by padres. But the life was not for me. But there I learned English as well as Spanish. I have a great affection for the Mexicans, especially for their horses." El Tigre's black eyes twinkled. A sense of humor, however brutal, Sundance thought. El Tigre continued, "The Mexicans honor me by naming me El Tigre. And so I shall remain. And now you will be given more food. And you must rest. Tomorrow when the sun is directly overhead, you will fight. It is the hour set by Many Wolves for this contest in blood."

"A contest in blood . . . to the death."

"The weapons you left with your horse have been taken. They will be returned when you are successful tomorrow."

Sundance was given a wickiup to himself. Food was brought to him—wild pigeons killed in flight by bird point arrows. The squaws treated him almost reverently. Thanks to Many Wolves, he seemed to be regarded as a god.

Anxious to make his first contact with Hunter and the girl, he wolfed down his food, then strolled about the camp, telling some suspicious braves that he wanted only to stretch his legs. They nodded, letting him go his way. He wanted to get the layout of the camp so as to plan his escape. He knew of the one trail and knew there must be another to this natural fortress high on the mountain. After unsaddling Eagle and turning him into the horse herd, there had been no chance to look around.

Camp dogs found his scent strange. They sniffed and one of them bared fangs. An old squaw shouted at them and they scampered away. She gave Sundance a toothless smile, which he acknowledged with a nod of his head. She seemed pleased.

Near one of the several metal cook pots he saw the Indian girl who had caught his attention earlier. She was bent over, using a long spoon to stir the contents of the pot. Her black braids interwoven with ribbons hung over her shoulders. She saw him and straightened up, hands pressed against her skirt of deerhide.

She said, "You must have food. El Tigre wants you strong for tomorrow."

He started to say that he had been fed, but she quickly placed a finger across her lips. None of the busy squaws nearby seemed to notice her signal for silence.

"Yes, I do need strength," he said gravely and returned to his wickiup, hoping the girl would bring him some message. After waiting impatiently for an hour, he decided something had caused a change of plan.

It was noon when he went out again. Twenty-four hours until he was to fight Burke Hunter to the death. Another hour passed as he wandered about the camp where there were more women than braves. Tonight there would be a full moon, too bright for a successful escape. He would wait until it was down. In the full dark of those hours between three in the morning and predawn he would take Hunter and the girl. How this could be accomplished he had no idea. But plans must be made and quickly. He hoped the Indian girl would be of some help. He felt let down when he saw no sign of her in the bustling camp.

Although he appeared to be free to move about the camp at will, he felt the tension among these desert Indians who had been forced to the mountains following the massacre of Eskiminizin's people. Eyes watched him. They had never met a Cheyenne before, much less one with white blood and hair the color of the captive woman they had named Sunflower.

When he tried to get to the north end of camp near the horse herd, he was waved away by armed guards.

He had just retraced his steps when he saw a brave burst into camp from the south trail, his pony lathered as it careened between towering spires at the entrance. It was Black Moccasin, who had defected from Cochise in order to join up with the former Army scout, Big Luke.

There was a flurry of excitement now by the wickiups of El Tigre and the medicine man. Black Moccasin was speaking to Many Wolves, who stood, bent over, head canted as he listened. Then El Tigre strode up.

Sundance tried to get closer in order to overhear what was being said, but evidently the chief had given orders for him to be kept away. He was pushed back toward one of the racks where antelope meat was being dried.

It disturbed and angered him to see how friendly El Tigre seemed to be toward the renegade Black Moccasin. He clapped him on an arm, nodded his head vigorously.

Black Moccasin hurried to his spotted pony, then vaulted onto the animal and flashed his gaze around the camp. He picked Sundance out among the squaws at the drying racks. Black eyes in the broad face gleamed with triumph. And then the Apache was sending his pony at a hard run down the steep and dangerous trail that led to the flat lands.

Sundance wondered at the urgency. It was a message being taken to Big Luke, of course. Several times during the next hour, Sundance tried to speak to El Tigre to see what was going on. Each time he was waved away by the chief's many guards.

Tension seemed to increase in camp since the visit of Black Moccasin to the Apache hideout. Sundance also felt the tension in his own body—and his frustration—for he had seen no sign of any white captive, either male or female. Where were they being held? In a wickiup, and never allowed outside?

A male voice spoke in English from behind one of the wickiups Sundance was passing: "Seems they have it set for noon tomorrow. Your blood or mine."

8

Sundance whirled. A white man, tall and lithe, stood next to one of the towering rocks at the mesa rim. Sundance did not hurry, but took his time so as not to attract attention. Burke Hunter stood with hands thrust into the pockets of work pants, an arrogant smile on his lips.

"Seems we're destined to fight," Hunter said, the arrogance of a smile also in the voice. "Your reputation with a knife is well known, Sundance."

"And yours." Sundance found it hard to hold himself in because he was thinking of tendons needlessly severed in the arm and leg of a Cheyenne youth.

"How the hell have you managed to stay alive?" Sundance asked.

"At first I thought I'd die by torture," Hunter said, misinterpreting Sundance's question. "But I used my wits when they brought me here. I bragged that I had a sacred knife that would protect me. Many Wolves believed me." Hunter looked him over with eyes almost as pale as those of an albino. He might have been handsome had it not been for the eyes and the cruel set of lips. Sundance could see why Eloise Hunter might have been attracted to him. Even in his torn and soiled shirt and pants and high laced miner's boots, he exuded a certain charm. He stood slightly taller than Sundance, with good shoulders and long legs.

Hunter said, "Let's walk and get away from these bastards." And when Sundance's eyes narrowed, Hunter smiled. "Only El Tigre and one or two others understand English."

They started walking, Sundance saying, "All of a sudden they don't care if we're seen together?"

"Things have changed in the last hour. Don't ask my why. Who can ever figure an Indian?"

They were walking in the direction of the horse herd at the far end of the hideout. Sundance casually mentioned the gold mine Hunter had found.

"In the first place it isn't a mine," Hunter laughed. His hair was ragged and brown; stubble of the same shade darkened his tanned jaws.

"If it isn't a mine, then what *did* you find?"

"There was a mine once, yes." Hunter explained that it had been in New Mexico, found by conquistadores. During an Indian uprising, a few of them had loaded all the gold into wagons and fled, not toward Mexico, where most of them had taken refuge, but to the west. Finally the gold became a burden; some of the wagons broke down and they hid the gold. Then they decided to rejoin their comrades in Mexico, after all, and come back for the gold when the uprising was quelled. They were massacred by Apaches.

Sundance said, "How do you know all this, Hunter?"

"Documents in Spanish found in one of the chests of gold nuggets."

"*One* of the chests? How many are there?"

"Many," Hunter said amusedly. "Too bad you'll never see them."

Sundance laughed coldly. "The greatest knife fighter of all time. Is that how you think of yourself?" They walked along the rim of the camp. It was a temptation not to pitch Hunter to the rocks five hundred feet below; a thousand in some places.

"There are no greater knife experts than the river men," Hunter said arrogantly. "I grew up among them. Had a natural talent. I was taken under the wing of a Frenchman in New Orleans. By the time I was fifteen I knew every trick that can be done with a blade. In our final engagement I could have killed my mentor. I decided to spare him."

They had reached the horse herd. Sundance spotted Eagle among the other horses. Sundance whistled softly. Eagle's head came up. He did not call the horse; it would upset the guards. But he did see his saddle and bedroll between two trees. But not his weapons.

Two braves spurred up, gesturing fiercely for them to stay back.

"Afraid we'll try and grab a horse and ride for it," Hunter said, that damnable smile curving his lips.

They started walking away from the horses, Sundance trying to mask his growing rage directed at the man strolling so nonchalantly at his side. "Listen to me, Hunter. What we have to do is make some plans to get out of here. And take the girl with us. Where the hell is she, anyway?"

Hunter laughed. "By this time tomorrow I'll have my own free ticket out of this hell-hole."

Sundance caught him by an arm and spun him around. "You seem damned sure of yourself, Hunter."

"Blood Knife is the name," Hunter laughed. Then his lips twisted. "Take your hand off my arm. If I had my knife with me, you'd have no fingers."

Sundance released him, not because of the threat but because some armed braves had started toward them.

"We'd better talk about gold," Hunter said, as the braves brandished carbines. "A safer subject. I want you to realize how clever I've been."

"Tell me," Sundance said through his teeth.

"You see, I'd heard rumors of this cache of gold. I ran into an old Mexican who had a map handed down from his great-grandfather. Well, I got the Mexican drunk and he showed me the map."

Sundance's smile was cold. "And the Mexican is your partner now, of course."

"Hell, you'd kill a man as quick as I would. You've got the rep for it, God knows. The map was fairly accurate. I literally fell into the cache." He chuckled. "Rotted timbers gave way and there I was. Rich as Midas." Hunter threw back his head, laughter roaring from the parted lips. Squaws nearby tanning hides looked startled.

"Your gold's not worth a pound of dust," Sundance pointed out, "if you're not alive to spend it."

"Oh, I'll spend it, Sundance. I've got plans. I'm a good politician. I've been laying the groundwork since the minute I found the gold. When I get out of here I may run for territorial governor. I could buy enough votes to assure victory."

"Eloise Hunter, wife of a governor," Sundance said, giving the arrogant face a sidelong glance.

For the first time Hunter seemed upset. "I hear Eloise hasn't been exactly alone since I've been a prisoner of these bastards."

"Big Luke the messenger brought you word?"

Hunter halted, glared at Sundance out of narrowed pale eyes. "I daresay Eloise poured out her generous affection on you also!"

"I've got a binding contract with the lady. Nothing more between us than that."

Hunter looked at him in surprise. "A contract?" Then he recovered his aplomb. "I, as her husband, will repudiate said contract."

"She might just end up a widow," Sundance said lightly.

Hunter laughed, then his mood changed. "I wouldn't be in this goddam fix if I hadn't taken nuggets to show Grimholdt. Can't keep his damn mouth shut."

"That assayer wouldn't talk."

Hunter kicked at some stones. "Maybe I did," he conceded in a rare admission of human frailty. "I got a little drunk after I saw Grimholdt."

A girl stepped abruptly from one of the wickiups in the company of two squaws. And with her was the Apache maiden who had caught Sundance's eye earlier in the day.

Lila Corey was tall, slim, wearing a brown dress that had been torn and mended with heavy thread. Her yellow hair was a darker shade than Sundance's. She saw Hunter and her light gray eyes were scornful. Then she looked at Sundance and her eyes widened.

He didn't know whether she intended to speak or not, but the squaws tugged at her arms, hurrying her away. The Apache girl followed them, not looking around as Sundance had hoped.

"Arrogant bitch, that Lila," Hunter muttered. "I hope he uses the whip on her. He's got a rep for it."

Sundance's jaw hardened; he had kept Hunter talking, hoping the man would let something slip. He had. "Let's hear the rest of it, Hunter." They halted, eyes locked. Black Moccasin's dramatic appearance in camp followed by Hunter's nonchalance, added up. When Hunter only glared at him, Sundance said, "She's been promised to Big Luke."

"Guess maybe I do talk too much," Hunter shrugged. "Should've kept my mouth shut."

"Wouldn't have made any difference. The idea's been growing on me. When's Big Luke coming here?"

"An hour after sunup."

"Two contests within a matter of hours," Sundance said coldly. "Big Luke. Then you with the knife."

"You poor damn fool, you'll never live to fight me."

Two braves appeared, shouting at Hunter, gesturing. He looked blank and looked to Sundance for translation.

"El Tigre wants you," Sundance said, and watched him hurry away in the company of the two Apaches. Sight of the man's arrogant walk was almost as sickening as having to listen to his braggadocio.

Sundance smiled coldly. Hunter might have other plans, but Sundance had no intention of leaving him behind to await noon tomorrow and the fight with knives.

On his brief inspection trip to the north of camp,

he had verified the fact that there was a second trail. He had seen two braves riding it from below. It was the route Sundance would take tonight in the dark of the moon.

Sundance hunted for the Apache girl and Lila Corey. He saw neither one. Time was running out. It was important that he win Lila's confidance. White clouds in the dry mountain air boiled about higher peaks to the north, and pulled into strange shapes by turbulence.

At last he found the girl, seated dejectedly on a flat rock. A squaw had finished rinsing soap from the long pale hair by sloshing water over the bent head. Sundance waited until the squaw had departed for more water, leather bucket thumping against a skirted leg, before approaching the girl.

"You're Sundance," she said, pushing aside the damp hair. "Moon Star has talked about you." Lila swallowed. "The washing of the hair . . . I'm being prepared for my new master."

"You'll have no new master." But she seemed not to hear him.

"Big Luke. I've seen him here in camp. His stare always turns me cold." She shuddered.

Sundance squatted beside a towering rock, one eye on the squaws and braves moving toward cook fires or horse herd.

"Lila, listen to me. Is Moon Star the Apache girl you were with?"

But again the girl seemed not to hear what he was saying. Her light gray eyes reflected bitterness. "You want to know how I met that terrible person—Hunter." Sundance started to interrupt, but it all boiled within her. He decided to let her talk. She told how her father found life confining on their ranch at

Whipple Creek, and wanted to take up land near the Rockies.

She choked up. "Oh, if he had only stayed. We had friends. Whipple Creek is the longest we stayed anyplace since my mother died. He was so . . . so restless."

"Why haven't your relatives worried about you? Or your friends?"

She said she had no relatives, and the friends they had made at Whipple Creek didn't expect word from them for months. She spoke of how their wagon was overloaded. "I sensed it was from the start. I think Dad knew it, but he wouldn't discard anything. We got mired in quicksand. When he tried to dig us out, he . . . he just fell over."

"And then Hunter happened along."

"I heard a horse. I was so distraught that I grabbed a rifle, thinking it was an Indian." She looked at him. "I didn't mean it the way it sounds. But I've been deathly afraid of Indians ever since we moved to Whipple Creek. About all the people talked about were the dread Apaches." She gave a despondent sign. "And here I am their captive." She drew a deep breath. "Burke took time to dig a grave for Dad. I did appreciate that. Burke let me have his horse, and we had just started out when we were surrounded."

He mentioned her use of the first name. "You're fond of Hunter?"

"At first. Because he came into my life at a time when I was desperate." She shuddered. "I changed when I saw him kill three men—the last one even worse than the other two. He cut him horribly. Worst of all, he seemed to enjoy it."

"Lila, we've got to make plans." He mentioned the Apache girl. "Can she help us?"

"Moon Star wants to help. She has to be very careful. She's going to try and get you a gun."

"Ahhh." Sundance's smile was fierce.

"She speaks English, of course. She's a bright girl and much too good to stay here for the rest of her days."

"Try and bring Moon Star here."

"I can't leave until the squaws get through with me." She looked him in the eye. "Moon Star says you're quite famous. A Cheyenne Dog Soldier and . . ." She broke off, reddening.

"Killer." He finished for her.

She ignored it. "Can we get out?"

He told her about making a break. An hour or so before dawn when the moon finally went down.

"Thank God," she said fervently. "I'd do anything rather than be a slave of that horrible Luke. And that's what Moon Star says it amounts to."

"We'll need luck, but we'll make it."

Her smile was tremulous. "And if we escape, you won't have to face up to morning. Some terrible test they plan for you . . ." She broke off, as two plump squaws came around a wickiup, talking to each other, each carrying a filled bucket.

"Bath water for me." Lila shuddered. "Luke's instructions for his bride to be, so I've been told." She stood up.

"They'll humor Luke on the chance he might win. But he won't." He smiled. "By the time he gets here, we'll be gone."

"You'd better leave now. If they see us talking together . . ."

"I'll be back in an hour." He hurried away.

He saw Hunter, the pale eyes gleaming, the arrogant smile pasted to the lips. "Even better than I thought. Big Luke will have help." He laughed. "It's no secret now. I can talk freely about the morning *test*." Hunter bared his teeth. "Too bad I won't be the one to kill you."

"When it's time for your killing," Sundance said angrily, "I'll remember a Cheyenne boy, and how you cut him to pieces in Newton, Kansas."

Hunter's look was blank. "Indian boy?" Then he remembered. "*That* kid. Well, I cut him so he'd always remember me."

"You son of a bitch!" Sundance cried.

Hunter sprang for his throat, but Sundance caught him by the wrists. As they swayed, locked together, two guards came at a run, brandishing carbines.

Not wishing to test their tempers or marksmanship, Sundance pushed Hunter away. He drew a deep breath, trying to get himself under control. The callous manner in which Hunter had referred to the Cheyenne youth had been too much.

Hunter stared at him. "If we do meet tomorrow by some miracle," he said, voice shaking, "I won't get it over quickly as planned. If you think I cut that Cheyenne kid, it's nothing to what I'll do to you before I rip out your guts."

Walking away, Sundance brushed past Moon Star. She pretended to be knocked off balance. As she righted herself she swung close. "Your weapons are in El Tigre's wickiup. I will try to get them."

Then she was gone. Sundance dared not show his sudden elation.

He was summoned to an audience with El Tigre.

The chief nodded to him, beckoned him closer and, surprisingly, laid an affectionate hand on his arm.

Hovering at the chief's back was the medicine

man, his eyes in the dark, lined face bright with anticipation. He was bent over, supporting his weight on a stout stick.

El Tigre mentioned the scars on Sundance's chest. "You have been put to the test before, Sundance of the Cheyennes. And those scars mean you were initiated into the Dog Soldiers. And so you will be put to the test here."

"An hour after sunup, I understand."

"It is time for you to go to your wickiup and contemplate your strength and your cunning. Many Wolves tells me that you are great medicine. And if you are put to the supreme test and are victorious, it will benefit my people. You will not fail me. And tomorrow at noon, after you have killed Blood Knife, I will look upon you as my son." El Tigre's voice rose. "You and Sunflower will live with us for the rest of your days. You are the medicine that Many Wolves said was sure to come to me." The voice trembled with emotion. "Your medicine and that of the sacred gold will mean that the pony soldiers will never again have power over us. We will sweep them and all the whites off our lands as a man tramples ants into the dust."

El Tigre turned his back and strode away; the audience was over.

At the far end of the camp Sundance paused to watch braves teaching some young how to handle a bow and arrow. It brought back his own youth, when he had been the prize pupil of his grandfather, the chief.

One of the teachers was no more than twenty, the age Sundance had been when he won his Cheyenne war bonnet.

The young brave looked at Sundance out of

bright eyes. "Many Wolves says that you can turn aside an arrow and even stop a bullet with the palm of the hand. And if this is so, you will be the greatest warrior among us." In awe the small boys with their bows and arrows stared at Sundance.

From a corner of his eye he saw Moon Star beckoning. He strolled away from the teachers and their pupils, then joined Moon Star in a narrow cleft between tall rocks where they were unseen by others.

Moon Star tilted her head so that bright sunlight brought out the sheen of her black hair. "Sundance, your weapons are well-guarded."

"You'll find a way," he said urgently.

"At the very least, I'll get you a gun," she promised.

"Don't take chances, Moon Star. I don't want you to get into trouble."

"I will take risks because Lila should be returned to her own people." She now spoke in Apache. "In some ways El Tigre is a fool to listen to Many Wolves. Some of the braves don't like him, but he hopes to win them over completely by this show he has promised them; the Cheyenne Dog Soldier will be pitted against the brutal fists of Big Luke, and later he will fight a duel to the death with Blood Knife."

Sundance leaned close. "We leave tonight."

Her eyes glowed with approval. "Leave when the moon is down. There are not many braves in camp. It is your chance to get away before the others return with horses from Mexico. Scouts say they are on their way. But when they will arrive, I have no idea."

"When we make the break, you come with us."

She said it was not possible. She intended to marry a brave, Three Rivers. He was returning with the raiding party. Sundance accepted that. He had one more request. If possible, he wanted her to get her hands on Burke Hunter's fighting knife.

Her teeth flashed, sensing his motive. "Now I must go. Before I am missed."

Sundance felt a rising excitement. He glanced at the clear sky. It was only two hours past noon, plenty of time left for her to retrieve his weapons or show him how it could be done.

As he was walking toward the cook fires he heard a sudden scuffing of moccasins at his back; men coming at a hard run. He started to turn, then felt his arms seized. An Apache on either arm. Although he hadn't seen these two up close before, he knew they were the pair who had been with Black Moccasin.

"Hold him, Crossed Arrows!" It was the Apache clinging to his right arm who shouted at his companion, flat-nosed and chunky. The one who had shouted was Two Trails, a brand of ownership on his forehead indicating that he had once been sold into slavery.

As Sundance started to twist free, Black Moccasin struck him from behind, pushing hard with both hands, all three of the Apaches propelling him toward the nearest cook fire at a stumbling run. It was either run with them or lose his balance and fall face down.

"Push his right hand in the cook pot!" Black Moccasin yelled.

With a mighty roar, Sundance flung off Crossed Arrows. But Black Moccasin at his back struck him behind an ear with a clubbed fist. Half-stunned, Sundance broke stride. Black Moccasin thrust out a leg, tripping him. Sundance fell hard. He bounded to his feet and fought them with point of elbow, but their combined weight was too much to handle. As he struggled up, pulling them with him, he freed an arm and smashed a backhand just under the brand on the forehead of Two Trails. The Apache's legs made a wishbone, then folded. But Black Moccasin and Crossed Arrows were both on his right arm, dragging him toward the pot boiling over the cook fire. Crossed Arrows, recovered from the backhand, began pushing him. Just as they were about to thrust his hand into the steaming liquid, Sundance, with sheer strength, flung them off. And at that moment he saw Big Luke in the crowd of Apaches now formed in a large circle. And Sundance knew the reasoning behind this treachery: Big Luke so determined to win Lila Corey and the sack of gold nuggets that he would go to any lengths.

And El Tigre had evidently sanctioned it. It was a sneak attack intending to cripple him, to make him even more vulnerable to Big Luke's mighty fists, to catch him off guard. El Tigre stood not a dozen yards away, arms folded. At his side the senile Many Wolves bent over his cane.

In that instant Sundance's head finally cleared from the clubbing he had received behind the ear and he shouted, "Cripple me, will you!"

With his perfect balance he sent Crossed Arrows and Two Trails tumbling into the dust as Black Moccasin tried to seize him around the knees. Sundance cupped his two hands, caught Black Moccasin under the chin, and flipped him backward toward the fire. One of Black Moccasin's feet kicked over the pot and its contents made a swath through the dust. Black Moccasin landed so close to the coals that the ends of his long black hair were singed.

He yelped and rolled aside, beating out one flicker

of flame near a shoulder. Crossed Arrows, in trying to get up, floundered in the pool of spilled food. It was a scene to evoke laughter, but the large circle of onlookers, braves, and the more numerous squaws and maidens were strangely silent, almost as if it might be a religious rite, instead of the treachery of three men against one.

9

Black Moccasin, half-stunned, on his knees, was rubbing at the singed ends of his hair. His gaze on Sundance was venomous. But the eyes also held a glint of triumph.

It was all the warning Sundance needed. He was suddenly aware of grunts, of the sounds of a big man coming at full stride. Glancing over a shoulder, he saw Big Luke at a hard run, intending to ram him into the fire pit.

Sundance started to run away from him and saw the look of disappointment on El Tigre's face. But it was only to get away from the spilled food. In a cleared space where the footing was better, he suddenly whirled, bracing himself. There was a great smacking sound of flesh against flesh as their bodies collided. Such impact would have shattered the bones of lesser men. They broke apart, circling slowly, two gladiators attired in breech clout and leggings. Luke had smeared his heavy torso with grease to make it difficult to sustain a hand-hold. As they wrestled across the campground, the odor of rancid grease was strong in Sundance's nostrils.

"My woman, my gold," Luke hissed as he tried to wrap his huge arms around the shorter Sundance's waist.

Sundance grappled with him, his hands slipping on the greasy flesh. "You don't know the meaning of fighting fair," Sundance flung at him as they swayed, locked together, in a circle.

"El Tigre says you're a spirit man," Big Luke taunted in Cheyenne, laughing. "The more odds against you, the greater the medicine. But you're only flesh and blood like the rest of us. When I beat you to death, then El Tigre will know which of us is the greater medicine."

From Sundance's throat came the blood-chilling war cry of the Cheyenne as Big Luke's arms tightened about his waist. Luke snorted in triumph; he believed the brawl was won hardly before it had started. His fingers locked against the spinal column; he began to bend Sundance back. Excitement danced in the eyes of the onlookers, as if they expected a quick finish, a snapped spine under the pressure of those powerful arms.

For the benefit of the stoic Apaches, Sundance glared defiantly up at the broad, scarred face above him, showing utter contempt. And to punctuate it, he broke the hold; a sudden upthrust of arms tore Luke's locked fingers apart.

Still showing the same contempt, Sundance thrust the bigger man aside, danced back out of range of Luke's giant fists swinging at his head. Luke pressed relentlessly, teeth bared.

"You got away from me that time, Cheyenne!"

Luke shouted. "Next time I'll crack your spine like a stick!"

In the midst of his raging threats Luke took a solid smash to the jaw. His body shuddered. In other savage encounters such a tremendous blow would have ended it. Luke's legs, as if made of iron wood, somehow stiffened and propelled the body suddenly forward. Luke's knuckles with the scarred tissue grazed Sundance's chest instead of the jaw. No grizzly had ever exhibited more rage than Luke when the blow missed. And he did fight like a grizzly now, lashing out with both hands. Sundance spun away, chopped a right to the chin point, then followed with a left. But he suddenly chilled when he saw that Black Moccasin had recovered and was watching the battle from a few feet away, crouched on all fours in the position of a wild animal ready to spring.

In trying to keep Luke's ally always in sight, Sundance nearly became trapped again in the power vise of Luke's arms. Sundance clawed at the forearms before they could lock in place, fingers slipping on the greasy skin. Luke tried again and succeeded.

"I promised Hunter I'd have your brains in the dust, Cheyenne," Big Luke snarled.

In close, Sundance brought his forehead sharply down, hoping to smash the nose. All he got was the tip. But the blow to the sensitive spot brought a howl from Luke and a loosening of the terrible arms.

Sundance tried to pull away. Luke rammed a thumb at an eye, but Sundance jerked aside in time. His hard right to Luke's rib cage traveled only a few inches, but Luke's jaw dropped, the eyes flooded with pain. Another smash to the ribs and Sundance was rewarded by Luke's grunt of pain and surprise. Sundance ducked and weaved and struck again and again when the mighty fists missed their target. Another war whoop burst from Sundance; no Cheyenne in battle had ever sounded more confident. He was proving himself before El Tigre. A fight to the death, for sure, but Big Luke was already in trouble. Most men, upon witnessing such an historic contest, would have given vent to their feelings. But not a sound came from the watchers, as the two bronzed and sweated giants tried to batter each other into oblivion.

Not a one of them, including their chief, seemed outraged when Black Moccasin decided it was time to give the faltering Luke a hand. He suddenly hurled himself at Sundance's ankles. Sundance was toppled. As he was falling, he somersaulted across the hardpan, righted himself, momentum carrying him into a dead run. He twisted aside and spun back on Black Moccasin about to regain his feet. A startled look crossed the Apache face now on a level with Sundance's lifted knee. At a hard run, Sundance drove it into the face of the rising Black Moccasin. Blood spurted from crushed lips. Sundance stumbled over the unconscious renegade, regained his balance, and whirled.

He expected Luke's cohorts, Crossed Arrows and Two Trails, to rush him also. But he saw them, ringed by Apaches, staring sullenly. No doubt restrained on El Tigre's orders. Obviously the chief had a macabre sense of fair play.

As Sundance scrubbed a forearm across his sweated face, something hit him from behind. He found himself face down in the dirt, dimly aware that Luke was astride his back. He felt Luke's greasy fingers slip around his neck, reaching toward the throat. When the fingers tightened, black dots began to flicker. In another few seconds those bruising fingers would squeeze out the last thread of consciousness. Then Luke could leisurely beat him to death in front of the silent onlookers.

In desperation, Sundance gave a mighty heave of his body, toppling the big man. Sundance sprang up, rubbing at the bruised throat. He gulped at the thin mountain air. Luke remained down for only a moment, giving Sundance no opportunity to recover from the near-strangulation. Big Luke seemed to sense victory and his grin split the sweated, bloodied face. His triumph was short-lived, however. Sundance swarmed in with dazzling speed, smashing rights and lefts at the great hulk. Even the Apaches seemed awed that he had recovered so soon from near disaster.

In frustration, Luke suddenly scooped up a sharp-edged stone from the fire ring and tried to rake open the initiation scars on Sundance's chest. Sundance struck Luke's wrist with such force that the rock spun into the crowd of onlookers, narrowly missing El Tigre, who now watched the battle with unconcealed interest.

"Stand still and fight, Cheyenne!" Luke cried.

A tremendous right under the heart whitened Luke's lips. He staggered, moaning. The arms dropped suddenly in order to protect the midsection from further punishment, which gave Sundance the jaw as target. Even with every ounce of body weight behind the blow, Luke only wavered but did not go down.

Desperately Sundance pursued him. Through the haze of dust lifted by their moccasins, he saw Lila

Corey on tip-toe, face dead white, a forearm across her lips as if to stifle a scream. Nearby was Burke Hunter, scowling, the arrogant smile for once missing from his lips.

Cupping hands, Hunter shouted at Big Luke. "For Christ's sake, *finish* him!"

Luke, wavering, cursed him in Apache, which Hunter did not understand. A few of the Apaches nudged one another. One of them actually smiled.

As the combatants slugged it out, Hunter tried again. "Luke, remember the girl! And the gold!"

The shouting seemed to penetrate Luke's befuddled senses. Thrusting aside Sundance's left jab, he lunged desperately, his face drained from the pounding Sundance had directed at his midriff. A roundhouse swing whipped an inch from Sundance's headband. And as Big Luke came around, off balance, his jaw met a crushing uppercut. Luke's eyes crossed, seemed to glaze.

Utter silence fell over the camp, broken only by faint sounds from the horse herd bunched to the north against towering slabs of rock.

Although Sundance longed to sit in the shade and have someone pour cool water over his throbbing skull, he stood straight as a war lance. He strode around the great circle as if fresh, staring at each face in turn. Upon reaching El Tigre, he read frank admiration in the eyes. Lila Corey seemed gripped by nausea but managed a faint smile. Moon Star inclined her dark head to Sundance, indicating her approval. Burke Hunter wore a look of utter amazement.

El Tigre crossed over to Sundance. The chief, a shorter man, had to reach up to place a hand on Sundance's shoulder.

"You are a true warrior, Cheyenne," he said fervently in Apache. "Now that you have vanquished that Big Luke, the medicine is doubled. Because tomorrow you face Blood Knife. He will be fresh, while you will still be bruised and battered from your supreme test today. Even so, you will be the victor."

"I will do my best."

"It is ordained," El Tigre said, black eyes dancing. "Surely you understand that, Sundance."

Lila Corey suddenly tore herself away from the guarding squaws. Skirts flying, she rushed toward Sundance, sobbing his name. Before she could fling her arms around Sundance, El Tigre blocked her.

"Tomorrow you are his woman, not today," El Tigre said sternly. She looked blank. She did not understand Apache. Just as well, Sundance felt.

She was led away but turned to give Sundance a stricken look before she was lost to sight in the maze of wickiups strung across the west side of this isolated fortress mesa.

After beating Luke, he was treated with more consideration, obviously on the chief's orders. A squaw brought him water. He drank deeply, then washed off sweat and grease. He knew that in defeat he had in Big Luke an even greater enemy than before. He had deprived Luke of his prize, woman and gold. There was talk that El Tigre might order him killed or banished. Greater irony would be to somehow turn him over to the Army, where the delayed gallows sentence could finally be carried out.

Thinking of Big Luke reminded Sundance of what the man had said about seeing him some years before at Bent's Fort. In his let down after the savage brawl, stretched out on blankets in his shadowed wickiup, it all came flooding back on him; the day that had changed him from Cheyenne warrior to half-white, half-Indian avenger.

On that long ago day, Sundance had visited the fort with his parents who had come to sell hides. Because of horse races, he had asked permission to remain behind; he would catch up with his parents later.

His father had laughingly indulged him, then left the fort with Sundance's mother, Smiling Woman. They had been gone only an hour when Sundance learned that a horse thought to be the fleetest of foot turned out to be the sorriest. With empty pockets, he hurried to catch up with his parents, knowing that his father had purposely allowed him to learn a lesson concerning white man's foolishness.

Circling buzzards was the first indication of the horror he came upon some minutes later; his parents crumpled in death. Sight of the bodies and the obvious violation of his mother by the killers blinded him with grief and rage. After forcing himself to attend to the ritual for the dead, he looked for a sign: three bootprints left by moccasins. His mind reeled back to Bent's Fort, remembering three half-drunk Indians and their equally intoxicated white friends, former mountain men, once men of great pride. It was why the remark by Big Luke concerning his own father, a mountain man, had chilled Sundance in his camp at the cul-de-sac.

Sundance took the trail of the six murderers. The trail branched into six. A thousand miles and a year before he tracked down the last one. This one begged as had the others, on hands and knees.

"Was drunk, didn't know what I was doin',

Cheyenne!" screamed the grovelling white man. "I never touched the woman, your ma. Honest to God, I never touched her. It was the others!"

Sundance's smile was a terrible thing to see as the former mountain man made one desperate attempt to save his life by pulling a knife from his boot top. Sundance cut him. As the man screamed for mercy, he cut him deeper. Again and again. When finally the man pleaded to be put out of his misery, Sundance only prolonged it.

After that, he found that whiskey helped blank out the horror. And when he came out of the fog and realized some of the acts he had committed when under its influence, he limited himself to two drinks at a time. It was later that he embarked upon his new career: he hunted men for pay, not for vengeance, as with the six who had cut down his father, subjected his mother to terror, and then shot her in the head.

Since that tragic day north of Bent's Fort, he never discounted the part sheer luck played in the dangerous games he had elected to play. A man fighting for his life needed the advantage of every break in order to survive.

And the wise man sometimes made his own luck—as Sundance intended here in the Apache camp of El Tigre.

10

Having applied herbs and ointments supplied by squaws to his wounds, he strolled about the camp. Although no one seemed to be watching him, he knew that should he approach either of the trails, he would be blocked. He could go only so far. He might be in El Tigre's favor at the moment, but it could change in the wink of an eye should he boldly attempt escape.

He kept eyes and ears open as he moved about the rock-ringed fortress, overhearing snatches of conversation in Apache. He heard again about a majority of the braves returning from the great horse raid into Mexico, which was all part of El Tigre's plan to ignore other Apache chiefs, recruit as many of their followers as possible, and go on his own, listening only to the counsel of the ancient medicine man, Many Wolves. El Tigre's belief that he was destined to lead the Apache nation to victory made him all the more dangerous, subjecting his followers to great risks in the foolish venture. Sundance knew from experience that if El Tigre persisted, he would feel the full might of the U.S. Cavalry.

Later that afternoon he had a chance to expand on this to Moon Star, when they met again in the cleft of rocks. The pony soldiers, he said, might be green troopers, but in an emergency veterans of the recent struggle between North and South would be recalled in an all out war against the Indian.

"El Tigre is headstrong," the Apache girl whispered. "And I certainly do not believe in things like sacred gold."

"Don't cast aside all the beliefs of your people," he cautioned.

"Oh, I believe in most of them. But I've lived around whites, and I know their thinking." She spoke again of her husband-to-be who was on the horse raid. "When he returns, I will be his bride."

"This is what you want?" he asked, sensing hesitation.

"If it were not for him . . . perhaps . . ." She looked into Sundance's coppery features, then lowered her eyes. "A part of me would like to escape with you and Lila. But the other side of me reminds me I am Apache, that I have promised myself to a warrior." She put a hand on his arm. "Lila Corey would make a good woman for you, Sundance."

Sundance shook his head. "No place for a woman in my life, because it might be a decade before I can help bring any real peace between Indian and white." Then he sighed. "With luck it might not be that long." His right rib cage still pained and he had trouble swallowing because of the bruised throat.

Moon Star was bitter. "Why can't we have peace

now? So I can live with my husband and have children without fear."

"Because the whites wanted to move West. They spilled across our lands like ants. Things could have been worked out." His lips curled. "There were treaties . . ."

"Pony soldiers broke every one."

"Not all pony soldiers are out to put the Indian in his grave." He knew this to be fact. Of course, others felt that the only good Indians were those who had not survived their mother's womb.

One heartening bit of news in his brief talk with Moon Star was that she had set aside a rifle for him. She had planned on a revolver, but this seemed impossible. She still hoped by some miracle to get her hands on his own weapons if El Tigre's guards became careless.

She gave Sundance a tremulous smile, then slipped away to take her place with other women at cook fires and drying racks.

It was shortly afterward that a half-dozen braves suddenly left camp by the south trail, raising a great cloud of dust. He hunted for Moon Star, hoping she could tell him what was happening. But she was still busy at the drying racks. She gave a slight shake of the head, and he knew she couldn't talk.

He hoped she might join him at their meeting place. She didn't come. As shadows began to lengthen, his tension increased.

At last she came. No, she didn't know what departure of the braves meant. The women had not been taken into El Tigre's confidence. But she said that Lila was ready to meet him around three in the morning, when the brilliant full moon would be gone at last. Even with most of the braves away from camp on the horse-stealing expedition, and this latest group pounding off on some undisclosed mission, the odds against a successful escape were still overwhelming.

Sundance had just returned to his wickiup when he heard someone outside whisper his name. It was Burke Hunter.

"Come in," Sundance hissed. "But if you try anything with a gun or a knife, I'll snap your neck."

"Hell, they won't even trust me with a slingshot." Hunter ducked to enter the low doorway, then straightened up to stare at Sundance in the dimness. He mentioned the Apache braves who had left camp in such a hurry. "Any idea what El Tigre's up to?"

"No."

"You think it's a hunting party?"

"Unlikely, this late in the day."

Hunter leaned close and said cautiously, "If you're making plans to escape, I want to go along."

Sundance kept a straight face. He didn't trust Hunter enough to reveal plans. But the man was going with them, as Sundance had intended from the first. By force if necessary. Sounds of camp filtered into the wickiup; barking dogs, whinnying of horses.

"We fight tomorrow as planned," Sundance said coldly. "El Tigre feels that the more odds I overcome, such as whipping Big Luke..."

"Christ, and you did whip him," Hunter interrupted with grudging admiration. "The bastard bragged that he'd never been beaten."

"You counted on it."

Hunter shrugged. "Sure I did. If he spilled your brains, he'd have had his reward, gold and Lila. And be in a position to ask a favor of El Tigre, to get permission for me to leave camp with them."

"How much did you promise Luke? Half the gold in that cache?" And when Hunter nodded, Sundance said, "The minute he found out where the gold was, he'd cut your throat."

"All my life I've lived by my wits, Sundance. I'll figure some way to survive." His lips curved in the familiar arrogant smile. "And, incidentally, make myself one of the richest men in the territory."

"The Apaches will never let you have that gold."

"I have friends. I should have confided in them instead of trying to keep it all for myself."

Sundance smiled coldly. "Greed. A short path to the grave."

"If I'd had my friends with me the day of my capture, I wouldn't be here. I did leave myself vulnerable by taking time to rescue Lila."

"Better to have left her with a dead father and ruined wagon, I suppose."

"They'd have all gone into the quicksand eventually."

"And they call the Indian cold-hearted," Sundance said.

Hunter laughed. "We're alike, Sundance. Hell, if we weren't ready to kill friend or enemy at the bat of an eyelash, we'd have both been dead long ago."

"Enemies I kill. Never friends."

"I can't figure you. Or any Indian." Hunter scowled. "If the damn Apaches hadn't made periodic checks on that gold . . . Well, they knew somebody had stumbled onto it. They kept watch. I saw them a couple of times but got away. That's why I decided to drive some horses up there. If I got in trouble, I figured I'd make 'em a present. I'd always heard that Apaches had no use for gold, but horses they prized above everything else."

"This happens to be their sacred gold. That makes a difference."

"You're smart for an Indian, Sundance. Most waste time with war dances and listening to a medicine man. But you think like a white man."

"I get it from my English father."

"I keep forgetting you've got white blood. You look so damn Indian. But that yellow hair should remind me." Hunter gave a deep sigh. "Almost wish I didn't have to knife you to death tomorrow," he said with a wicked smile.

You won't, Sundance wanted to say. In the dimness of the wickiup his eyes locked with the pale ones. Hunter didn't know it, but by three in the morning he'd come awake with a gun in his back. This time he'd be the hostage not of El Tigre, but of Sundance, the Cheyenne Dog Soldier.

There was a sudden great clatter of hooves. Sundance ducked outside and saw braves running toward the north end, women hurrying behind them. Children and dogs joined in the excitement. Cook fires gleamed in the twilight.

"What the hell's going on?" Hunter demanded at his elbow, but Sundance, unable to stand the sight of him any longer, quickly joined the crowd. He saw some braves he hadn't seen before, sweated faces showing signs of fatigue. They were pushing a band of horses up the north trail, turning them in with the other horses. He heard Eagle's trumpeting, the big appaloosa objecting to sharing grass with newcomers.

Sundance overheard snatches of conversation

from passing braves: "They have returned . . . six hundred head of horses . . ."

Moon Star drifted to his side unobtrusively, pretending to be as excited as the others. She spoke softly in English, her voice tight with worry.

She had just learned that earlier that afternoon a messenger had brought word to El Tigre that the horse-raiding party was near. Riders had been dispatched to relieve the weary braves and help drive in the herd.

She said tensely, "In all this excitement I was able to get your weapons."

"Thank God."

"They're in your wickiup." Her eyes mirrored fear. "But you and Lila have no chance for escape." She began shouting her own welcome to the returning braves to allay suspicion.

"We'll escape," Sundance said above the tumult. More of the horses were coming uptrail. Because of the steep trail only a few head of half-wild Mexican horses could be driven up at a time, ghostly now in the full dark. Sundance swallowed. With the return of the raiders, the odds were against them. Somehow it had to be managed.

In the confusion he heard Moon Star's voice speaking English again. His heart sank when she said that all she had been able to get were his Colt and rifle. Something would be missing from his life if he had to leave without his other weapons.

"There are too many men," Moon Star said, the pretty face distraught. "You'll never get away."

"*Now*," he said fiercely. "Now is the only time I'll ever have!"

"Sundance, it's suicide."

"Get Lila to my wickiup. Please, Moon Star. It's

the only chance that girl will ever have to get back to her own people."

Some exuberant braves, defying their weariness, came at a hard gallop down the hardpan, scattering laughing children and barking dogs, showing off to the delight of the women.

When the cavalcade had swept past, Sundance saw Moon Star through the dust cloud, hurrying away. If she couldn't get Lila, then he'd have to go for her himself.

He had just started on long legs toward his wickiup when Burke Hunter appeared. "You were talking to Moon Star. I overheard one word. *Now*. What'd you mean?"

Sundance thought quickly. "Got something to show you," Sundance said in a conspiritorial tone.

"Show me what?" Hunter demanded, falling in step.

"You don't know Apaches. I do." He made it sound vital. "Come or not. Suit yourself."

Sundance hurried on ahead, Hunter trailing. If his weapons were inside as Moon Star claimed, the first step of the escape could be managed. If for some reason they weren't, then he'd have to silence Hunter with his bare hands and leave him behind. That wouldn't be easy; the man was wiry and tough and already on his guard.

In the hubbub of welcoming the returning braves no one seemed to notice the hurrying Sundance. Braves who had remained behind were whooping their welcome, some even firing carbines in the air until someone shouted not to waste ammunition. Small boys dodged the racing horsemen as another band came pounding the length of the camp and back, hooves and their war cries filling the early dark.

Sundance ducked to enter his wickiup, every nerve filled with tension. His gaze flicked desperately around the shadowed wickiup. At first he saw no weapons and his heart turned cold. Then in the shadows he picked out a lump hidden under a blanket. In one lunge he was across the hard-packed dirt floor as Hunter entered the doorway. Sundance bent low, jerked aside the blanket, and saw his Colt and Henry rifle. He scooped up the Colt and whirled. "Hunter, you open your mouth," he told the surprised knife fighter, "and I'll blow your head off. You're coming along."

Hunter's teeth flashed in the gloom. "Bravo. Lead the way. I'm with you if you think we've got much of a chance."

"Not much. But it's worth the try."

Hunter leaned down. "I'll take the rifle . . ."

"Get your hands off it," Sundance warned. Hunter protested that he should have a weapon. Sundance was adamant. Not trusting the man, Sundance thrust the Colt into Hunter's back and herded him outside, the Henry rifle covered by a blanket of dull red stripes in his left hand. Although Hunter muttered protests, he had the good sense to obey.

Crouched by the wickiup wall in deep shadow, away from the celebrants, Sundance impatiently counted off the minutes. If for some reason Moon Star was unable to bring Lila, then he'd have to take Hunter along and go for her himself, which would only add to the already overwhelming odds. Moonlight now compounded them.

In the wide clearing that ran the length of the camp, between the east rim and the wickiups strung along the west rim, were milling horses and weary braves who had successfully raided into Mexico and returned all that way with little rest. There were shouted questions from those who had remained in camp and exuberant replies from the raiders.

In the excitement no one noticed the yellow-haired Cheyenne and the white knife fighter, known to the Apaches as Blood Knife. They stayed unmoving in dust and shadows, Sundance straining for a hopeful first glimpse of Moon Star and Lila.

Suddenly he saw two women who had had to wait while another band of raiders made their plunging run the length of the camp; warriors proving their endurance, stretching it to the limit, this exhibition of manhood for the benefit of women and those braves unfortunate enough to have had no part in the raid.

And when the horsemen had dashed on with shouts and a roaring of hooves, the two women came at a fast walk. One was Moon Star, carrying something. The other was Lila, wearing a heavy shawl to hide her yellow hair.

Moon Star reached him first, and when he saw his precious *parfleche* bags his heart sang. These barely covered by a blanket. And over her shoulders, also covered by a blanket, were his cartridge belts, his holster, and sheathed Bowie knife. With an exultant cry he leaned over and kissed Moon Star's cheek, which brought her head around so that their lips met. Her eyes, which he could barely see in shadows and great clouds of dust, were large with surprise and pleasure.

He handed Moon Star his rifle. "If Hunter makes a wrong move, shoot him."

"You can trust me," Hunter protested. Sundance ignored him and quickly buckled on his belts.

Moon Star led them along a path through the

rocks, through a narrow slit between towering boulders, and then to a narrow trail at the mesa rim. A full moon brightened the canyon floor far below. Sundance cautioned the two girls against a misstep that could send them hurtling over the edge. They hurried single file along the rim, Moon Star in the lead, followed by Lila and Hunter, the latter making more noise than the rest with his heavy miner's boots. Sundance brought up the rear, carrying *parfleche* bags and rifle.

Moon Star reached the end of the protective rocks. She hesitated. From here on they would be in the open.

Another two dozen head of horses were being driven up the north trail, the weary raiders thundering to the mesa. And then as the others had done, they galloped the length of the camp. There were more shouting and war cries. More loose horses reached the camp and suddenly began to panic in all the noise and confusion. A brave on foot was knocked down, and several squaws had to run for their lives, skirts soaring. But their laughter belied their fear. And even the brave who had been knocked down picked himself out of the dust, grinning, his nose bloodied.

Watching her chance, Moon Star scampered along the edge of the milling herd where Eagle stood out among the other horses. Sundance's shout brought the appaloosa's great head up. And then it was charging through the excited horses, nipping those not moving quickly enough out of its way.

Sundance remembered where he had seen his saddle and bedroll. Sundance handed Moon Star the rifle to keep Hunter covered while he quickly saddled, then gestured at Hunter.

"Pick yourself a horse!" Sundance shouted above the din. Then he turned to Moon Star. "Sure you won't come with us?"

The Apache girl shook her head.

"I understand," Sundance said and took precious seconds to grip her arm and say, "Without you we couldn't have made it." And he almost added, we might not even make it now. But he was not given to pessimism. He leaned down, hugged the girl, and kissed her on the lips. "Much luck, Moon Star."

He couldn't be sure because of the dust that by now soared skyward to shade the moon, but he thought there was a hint of tears in her eyes.

From the shouts in Apache he realized the last of the stolen horses had been driven to the mesa; the north end was jammed with them. There were more shouts now and reckless carbine fire.

"Lead the way, Hunter!" Sundance ordered, pointing at the trail that dropped abruptly from the rim.

And as Sundance swung Lila up behind, Hunter started to argue.

"Get moving, damn it," Sundance shouted. "We..."

It was all he got out. He was recognized. The returning raiders had not seen him before, but directly ahead, acting as guards, were the two Apache sentinels who had been on the lookout ledge when he arrived in camp.

The nearest of the Apaches, a blob of squat shadow on the back of a pinto, shouted a warning, unheard above the pounding of the many hooves, the shrill whinnying of the stolen horses. He thrust at Sundance with a war lance. Lila screamed. But his lance point was knocked aside. Sundance seized the lance and slammed its butt end against the jaw, dumping the Apache.

The second Apache aimed a carbine. It flashed muzzle fire in the moonlight, but Sundance's Colt spoke an instant sooner. A scream of pain came from the brave as the right arm flopped crazily. More outcries erupted from the campground, everyone suddenly alerted.

"Hang on!" Sundance shouted back at Lila, who clung with both hands to his belt.

Even as the words left his lips, the great Eagle was at full stride plunging almost straight down on the dangerous trail. Where it widened slightly, the appaloosa thundered past Hunter on the Indian pony.

Sundance shouted back at him. *"Hurry!"* He didn't know if Hunter heard him above the pound of hooves, the war cries, and sporadic rifle fire from above. Hunter leaned over the neck of the pony, ragged hair blowing. Riding bareback under such circumstances was no mean feat for a white man. Much as Sundance hated him, he had to give the man a shred of grudging respect.

Pursuit was quickly organized. A dark blob of moving shadow, where the overhang cut off moonlight, now swept down on them. Warriors were now riding as recklessly as the escapees.

Something whirred past Sundance's left ear. An arrow quivered ahead in a mesquite beside the trail. Intermittent spurts of light came from above; bullets thumping into cactus and ironwood and sometimes screaming off slabs of rock.

Sundance in the jolting ride was thankful the trail was no wider, that it was purposely narrow to make it more easily defended. It was unsuitable for offense, as pursuers were beginning to realize. They had to ride single file and there was no chance to spread out and perhaps sweep in on them from the flanks. Never had Sundance seen such reckless riding as exhibited by the pursuing Apaches. Before, he had always considered Comanches to be the greatest horsemen in the southwest.

He heard Lila cry out as a mesquite branch whipped across her thigh. But she clung gamely to his belt. She was his greatest concern now. He and Hunter would have to take their own chances if recaptured; perhaps being staked out on an ant hill was the least of it.

"Pegasus! Every damn one of those Apache horses has got wings!" Hunter's voice faintly reached him from ten yards back. "They're *gaining!*" Hunter cried.

Reference to Greek mythology and the flying horse Pegasus was not lost on Sundance. He felt Lila's fingers tighten on his belt as she clung desperately to keep from being pitched off the back of the flying Nez Perce war horse.

At an abrupt widening of the trail, Sundance had a clear view of pursuers. Behind them came the Apaches single file through a deep cleft in towering rocks. If he ever had a chance to give them running room, it was now. Twisting in the saddle, he fired into the breastbone of the lead pony. In the hazy moon glow he saw horses crash into each other, riders catapulted into the air. A second group of riders smashed into the pileup. And as Apaches tried desperately to reorganize pursuit, the whole trail blocked now by sprawled men and horses, Sundance reached the canyon. Waving Hunter on, he swung south through the long slot. Stars glittered in a dustless sky, and moonlight was undimmed.

In the next hour they heard sounds of pursuit, but they were faint. Finally Sundance began to pick out landmarks. He recognized the terrain where he had herded Big Luke toward El Tigre's camp. He avoided his cul-de-sac, however, but found water at the side of another mountain.

Hunter wore his arrogant grin. "Brainless Apaches. We outsmarted 'em."

Hunter lost his grin when, after eating dried meat Lila had brought along, Sundance tied him in sitting position to a tree.

"No way to treat a white man!" Hunter raged.

"Not much of a white man," said a tired Lila, keeping him covered with the rifle Sundance had handed her.

11

In the morning, Sundance, still in breechclout and leggings, tested Hunter's bonds, then went hunting with bow and arrow. Whatever game he found would be slain soundlessly. It was barely light, the last stars beginning to dim. He was lucky and found game. As he neared camp, carrying a small antelope on his back, he heard Hunter's pleading voice.

"Lila, cut me loose."

"He said for me to shoot you if you try anything. And I will."

"I know I hurt you at the Apache camp because I put my own safety before yours. I apologize. Listen to me closely, Lila. I've got friends. One of them a gunhand named Bev Hatch . . ."

"Bev? A woman gunhand?"

Hunter burst out laughing. "A man, for Christ's sake. Yeah, his parents named him Beverly. A man ever call him that and the man is dead." Hunter's voice hardened as Sundance paused in the trees to listen. "Hatch moved in with my wife, I know that. From Black Moccasin's description it was him. But he knows every renegade in the territory. He'll round up some men, and we'll drive off the Apaches guarding my gold, and . . ."

"*Your* gold." Lila shook her head and shifted the heavy rifle. "Apache gold, Moon Star says. Certainly not yours."

"Mine. Listen to me, Lila. You can't trust a Cheyenne. And a half-breed is the worst of the lot. There's no difference between Sundance and Big Luke. Now please untie me . . ."

Sundance appeared with the antelope on his back. Hunter began to curse, but Sundance ignored him and built a smokeless fire. When the meat was cooked, Sundance freed one of Hunter's hands so he could eat.

Sundance broke camp, then freed Hunter. The usually handsome face betrayed strain, the eyes bloodshot, the mouth pinched. His clothing was torn, soiled.

It was shortly after dawn when they were in the saddle again. Sundance knew that with the coming of light, El Tigre would be hunting their sign.

Hunter spoke of the gold. "Sundance, you and me could end up owning half the territory." He spoke of the chests of gold reached by a vertical shaft that had been sealed off with heavy timbers covered with rock and dirt. "Luckiest day of my life when those timbers gave way and there I was. Rich."

"Apaches believe the gold is sacred," Sundance reminded.

"They're nothing but superstitious savages . . ."

"Seems to me the white man is as superstitious in his own religions as we are in ours," Sundance said coldly.

"Perhaps," Hunter said. He was in the lead astride the Indian pony. Not such a grand figure as when he had strutted about the Apache camp. Hunter said, "You told me you have a contract with my wife. I accept that. It means you'll have to know where to put your hands on the gold. I'll take you there. We'll talk about making a deal when we see the gold. Agreed?"

Lila, riding behind Sundance, whispered, "Don't trust him. He's such a smooth talker."

Sundance smiled to himself but nodded his head to show he appreciated her concern.

It was one of those spring days that suddenly became scorching. All that morning they pushed east in growing heat that sent even desert mice for cover, heading toward the great tumbled stretch of arid mountains some miles from Si Devlon's impregnable fortress. But it was not so impregnable, after all.

Already aching from the momentous struggle against Big Luke yesterday, the heat was further punishment. But he bore up without complaint. However, Lila was suffering. He could hear her occasional moans of exhaustion.

"How much farther, Hunter?" Sundance demanded. At times he felt as if the inside of his head shimmered as did the mountains ahead.

Hunter glared back at Sundance. "Before I tell you one damn thing, we're going to settle it about the gold." A parched throat made his words as rasping as a file on iron.

"We'll settle when we get there. With our knives."

At first Hunter looked surprised. Then pleasure touched the red-rimmed eyes. "Now you're playing *my* game!" he exulted.

"And mine."

Hunter laughed, the sound causing Lila, seated behind Sundance, to shudder. Hunter said, "Settle it with cold steel; winner take all."

Sundance didn't waste breath in a reply. His main concern as they began to climb was Eagle. How much longer could the horse continue in heavy sand and heat with the double burden? In addition, Lila's murmurings of pain and weariness were more frequent.

His practiced eye scanned the wasteland ahead, seeking a welcome spot of green that would mean water. Before long they might have to resort to getting it in minute quantities from the cactus. But within minutes his hope for water had more substance because the terrain was changing gradually, the trail steepening. A cooling breeze from higher elevations tempered the heat.

In searching for greenery in the bleak landscape Sundance noticed a film of dust a mile or so to their right. A chill struck the pit of his stomach; he was thinking of Lila. Apparently Hunter had not noticed the dust. Only a trained eye would be able to detect the almost invisible haze against the intense blue of the sky.

El Tigre's men? No. Apaches would swarm in on the outnumbered fugitives, not keep pace with them a mile or so to the east. He thought they had outdistanced El Tigre, at least for the present. But there were other possibilities—Big Luke and the three renegade Apaches, or the red-mustached Hatch, who had been behind the sneak attack at Si Devlon's mine, and then had tried to "talk" while waving a flag of truce. Or it might be some stranger. Nothing like a whiff of gold dust to bring the snakes out of their holes, Si Devlon had said.

Sundance felt the increased tension. It seemed to reactivate the hurts suffered in the bloody confrontation with Big Luke. A long scraped place on his side began to throb and sweat burned the numerous abrasions elsewhere on his body. Heat and weariness from the savage brawl of yesterday threatened to muddle his thinking at a time when he needed every instinct in order to survive.

Hunter plodded on ahead, the sun blazing on his unprotected head. But they all suffered equally, being hatless. Lila, clinging to Sundance's belt, continued to make whimpering sounds. Somewhere ahead, he recalled, was a stage road, running east and west. And somewhere there had to be a stage station. He had to get Lila to safety. Any stage could eventually get her to friends at her former home in Whipple Creek. She was becoming a burden and he couldn't risk any diversion that might leave him vulnerable to Hunter. Even unarmed the man was still a threat if the back was turned.

After a few more miles, he no longer saw the dust haze. Was it hidden behind a row of peaked chocolate-colored hills to the east? Absence of the dust worried him almost more than actually seeing its faint haze against the burning sky.

Not too far ahead now were mountains, great ribs of granite so high their crown of trees seemed in miniature.

"We'll find water," Sundance assured Lila.

"I . . . I just can't go on . . . I need rest . . ."

That she had borne up all these torturous miles astride the broad rump of the appaloosa in the blazing heat was a miracle.

"Hang on for another few miles," he urged, and

waited tensely for her reply.

Hunter looked over his shoulder, hunched on the back of the plodding Indian pony. "She starting to give out?" he asked, sounding hopeful.

"It's not going to give you a chance to plan anything," Sundance snapped. "So forget it." He ordered Hunter to keep riding on ahead.

"You think this is the cavalry and you're giving me *orders*?" Hunter demanded querulously.

"Do what you're told. And shut up."

Hunter glared, but he did urge the pony twenty yards or so up the brushy trail that now was climbing rather sharply.

"Soon as we find water," he told Lila, turning his head to glance back at her weary face, "I'll get you to a stage stop. You're going home."

"I have no home, Sundance . . . I want to stay with you."

"There's got to be somebody in Whipple Creek who cares about you."

She rested her forehead against his back, her long yellow hair swaying to the movements of the horse. "Ralph asked me to marry him. But I . . . I thought my duty lay with Dad and his plans to homestead in Colorado." She made a small sound of dismay. "But it seems like a lifetime ago."

"It isn't, Lila, it's only a few weeks."

"I don't want to go back there, Sundance. I want to stay with you . . ."

He made his voice purposely rough. "I can't waste breath arguing." And he sensed her hurt, but it couldn't be helped.

Hunter was waiting at the top of a grade. "What were you two talking about?" he demanded. The stubble on his cheeks had turned to beard. Pale eyes in the drawn face seemed sunken.

"Keep riding," Sundance said. "Don't ask fool questions."

When they were climbing again, Sundance stood up in the stirrups, trying to spot some indication of water in the hills and canyons ahead. Instinct drew him west and north, where he felt there would be a drain off from the mountains. His luck held. Within half an hour he had uncovered a waterhole. Lila flung herself down, kneeling over the indentation in the baked earth that held no more than a gallon at best. Once drained it would be slow to fill. But it would suffice for their present needs.

"Drink in sips," he cautioned the girl.

He tied the weary horses to a mesquite so they wouldn't get to the water before Lila had her fill and could wash herself.

He jerked his head at a sullen Hunter. "Let's give her some privacy."

As they made their way through the screening brush, he decided that the dust he had seen should be mentioned. But he needed a few answers first. When he and Hunter halted, he told the man about having overheard a mention of Bev Hatch. "How long have you known him?"

Hunter's reddened eyes studied him speculatively for a moment. "Hatch and I worked the riverboats out of Vicksburg."

"Card slicks, I suppose," Sundance said scornfully.

"One way to make a dollar after the war."

"How close are you now?"

"Black Moccasin took my letter to the ranch. He came back and said there was a man there. He described Hatch. But you know that."

"You didn't answer my question. How close are you?"

"I may need that bastard's help before this is over with," Hunter said thinly. "But once it's done, I'll drive my knife so deep in his belly it'll split the backbone. Just why the hell all these questions about Hatch?"

"Somebody's been trailing us," he said in a low voice so as not to alarm Lila who was out of sight now in brush and boulders. "Either they gave up for one reason or another. Or their dust is hidden behind the hills."

Faint alarm crossed Hunter's face. "El Tigre?"

"I don't think so. He's too far back. I'm sure of it."

Hunter scanned the sky, then turned and faced Sundance. "You figure it might be *Hatch*?" He started to laugh, but the look on Sundance's face froze him.

"If it is Hatch and you try to throw in with him . . ." Sundance paused for effect, which wasn't lost on Hunter. "Point is this, Hunter. If we're jumped, let's think of Lila. But if I hand over my Colt and you try anything, I'll live long enough to blow that head right off your shoulders. You understand?"

"Why should I give a damn what happens to her?"

"Because she's a woman."

"Yeah," Hunter sneered. "Last night in your blankets she proved that."

"You were tied to a tree. You were too far away to know *what* went on . . ."

The first hint of trouble was trumpeting from Eagle, followed by Lila's scream of terror.

12

The sounds were chilling on the hot afternoon. Sundance whirled, putting his back to Hunter, and bounded through the brush, Colt drawn, his heart hammering. And as he crashed through the last thicket of mesquite before the clearing and the waterhole, he came up short at sight of the terrified girl in the hands of the Apaches. The chunky Crossed Arrows had her by one wrist. Two Trails, the slave brand on the sweated forehead, had her by the other. They pulled her arms wide from her body. To one side stood Black Moccasin, hardly recognizable because of the ruin Sundance's knee had wrought to his nose and lips.

But the real threat was Big Luke. He was on the roan, the bruised face split in a triumphant grin. He had ripped Sundance's own war lance from Eagle's saddle. He gripped it in one large hand, the knuckles raw from yesterday's fight. The point of the war lance was pressing at a spot betweeen Lila's shoulder blades.

"Drop your gun, Cheyenne," Luke ordered, "or you'll see the point of this lance bust clear through her chest."

Sundance, rigid in those few seconds, saw the growing terror in Lila, who was held so firmly in the grip of the two renegades. All Big Luke had to do was drub heels against the roan's flanks to send it at lunge that would drive the war lance clear through the girl's body.

"All right," Sundance said in a dead voice. "Do what you want with me. Leave her out of it. Turn her loose."

Hardly had he uttered the last word when he heard someone behind him. He started to jerk his head around when something crashed into the back of his skull, pitching him into complete darkness. How long he lay he did not know, but consciousness streamed in and out like a tide. He felt sand in his nostrils, mouth. It was sheer agony to turn his head even slightly so he could clear nostrils of sand and breathe.

He heard Big Luke speaking to Black Moccasin. "We saw wild bees upcanyon. Find their hive." Sounds of a horse moving away.

Then Hunter shouted, "Give me Sundance's gun! I'll blow off his goddam head!"

"You come close to tearin' it off with that rock you hit him with," Luke said. He came to stand over Sundance, his heavy frame cutting harsh sunlight. "I want Sundance alive."

"Give me a gun," Hunter begged.

"No gun," Big Luke said flatly.

Black Moccasin returned. "Not much honey," he said.

"Enough to draw ants." Luke's laughter was

chilling. "They'll eat through his guts so slow he'll likely still be alive by sundown."

"You fiends!" Lila screamed.

There was a sudden smacking sound of a hand on flesh, followed by her whimper.

Desperately Sundance tried to lever himself up from the ground, but the large rock Hunter had hurled against the back of his head had badly injured him. His skull felt as if the bit of an ax had been driven deep.

He felt himself dragged through the sand a few feet. Sun was directly above, burning into his unprotected face and deep into his throbbing skull. He felt small stirrings against his lower back; a tickling sensation of insects. A thumping sound of rocks pounding on stakes reached him while Luke watched his three renegades drive four ironwood stakes into the ground. Everything went black again. Then he came to, realizing that he was spread-eagled, wrists and ankles firmly tied with rawhide strips to each of the stakes.

Black Moccasin came to stand over Sundance, fury stamped on the ruined features. "Leave me behind with him, Luke," he begged in Apache. "With a knife, I'll do a better job than ants."

"We're movin' out," Luke snapped. "We got things to do before dark. I'll take Sundance's Colt an' his rifle. Looks like a good Henry. I'd like to claim his hoss, but I ain't fool enough to try an' ride it. I've heard stories about Sundance an' that Eagle."

"Moving out is a good idea, Luke," Burke Hunter put in with false eagerness. "Sooner we get to Padre Canyon, the better."

"So that's where the gold is."

"I planned for you to be my partner from the first. But things went wrong at camp and I . . ."

"We're partners, you bet," Luke assured him coldly.

"You'll have your half of the gold. And you've got the girl. Two things you really wanted."

"I ain't too sure about her," Luke said heavily. "Her out all night with you an' that damn Cheyenne . . ."

"As we're riding I'll tell you about her in Sundance's blankets," Hunter said.

"So!" Luke thundered.

"A damn lie," Sundance managed to say.

But his voice was so weak Luke didn't even hear him. Luke directed his venom on Lila. "I think I'll get tired of her quick," he snarled.

"Don't blame you," Hunter said almost jauntily. "I know I wouldn't want her after that Cheyenne had her all night . . ."

"I want her all right," Luke said with a cold laugh. "When I get through with her, then I'll let my men have her. When they get their fill, I'll sell her. She'll bring a thousand dollars at a place I know on the border, pretty gal like her."

"I think we better get out quickly," Burke Hunter said nervously. "El Tigre's been after us, you know."

"That fool sent men after *us*." The cold laughter. "Execution party. One was Black Moccasin's cousin. We talked them out of killing us."

"We should hurry," Hunter urged. "El Tigre's left a few men to guard the gold. We'll have to kill them . . ."

"We kill," Luke said and looked directly at a suddenly pale Burke Hunter. "And don't worry about El Tigre. He's far back . . . miles . . . I know." Luke pulled Lila up behind him on the roan. "You don't whine too much, mebby I'll wait a month before I sell you." He grinned broadly.

She made one last plea. "Can't I persuade you not to leave Sundance behind. I . . . I'll do anything you want, if only . . ."

"You'll do anything I want. No worry about that." Luke turned in the saddle to glare down at the spread-eagled Sundance. "In an hour your screams will frighten the rattlesnakes," he said. Then he gave Black Moccasin an order.

Sundance felt a sticky substance smeared over his belly. Upon finishing this brief chore, Black Moccasin licked honey from his fingers, then vaulted into the saddle. Sounds of their hard-riding departure filled the canyon. Eagle, being driven ahead of them, trumpeted in his anger. And then came a silence so complete that it assaulted the eardrums.

It seemed only moments later that Sundance, lifting his head, saw the first inquisitive ant crawl tentatively across his belly. Soon he would be joined by a myriad of voracious cousins.

Sundance strained his eyes against the intense sunlight, seeking a weapon. Only his war lance lay near the waterhole where Luke had hurled it after threatening Lila; but it might as well have been on the moon for all the good it did him.

Finally his head began to clear, his skull no longer reverberating like a war drum. He tried to moisten sandy lips. He spat out as much as he could, then tried to shout the Cheyenne word that always summoned Eagle. It came out as a hoarse whisper.

A sudden sharp pain caused his belly to twitch. Then another. Looking down, he saw that the original red explorer had been joined by others. Honey was the present lure, but when they punctured the skin and drew blood they and thousands of their cohorts would nibble away at his living flesh. Already the pain was annoying; soon it would be unbearable.

This time, when he made his Cheyenne call it was loud enough to carry. But there was no response; perhaps they had driven Eagle miles away. Thoughts of what might have happened to the horse turned him cold, and for the moment took his mind off the savage ants. He tried to think back. He had heard no gunshot, so they hadn't destroyed the horse by bullet. Perhaps they had cut its throat. He groaned, knowing Luke and the others were capable of such wanton destruction. But they had been in a hurry, and perhaps had not bothered. Thinking of Lila tonight in Big Luke's camp was equally upsetting. Even Hunter might join in the pleasure, although Sundance doubted if Big Luke would even allow him that much. Once the gold was located, Hunter would be dead anyway.

He shouted again. Eagle might have broken away from them, and could be a mile or two out in any one of a number of branching canyons.

Desperately he struggled with the lashings that held his wrists and ankles firmly to the stakes. There seemed to be not the slightest give in either the bindings or the stakes. Sweat beaded his forehead from the exertion, the throbbing in his skull once again intense. Sunlight beamed directly into his face; he had to avert his gaze or risk having the eyeballs seared. And in these passing seconds the multitude of savage mites on his belly increased. The pain was now constant.

Again he shouted his command to Eagle, his voice

echoing against the rocks, the frantic sound slamming back on him. The ants seemed undisturbed. How ironic, he thought in his desperation, that ordinarily he could sweep them aside with his hand, grind them into the dirt with his heel. But now they were the masters, he the fallen.

A sound of hoofbeats stirred him as his repeated call finally ceased pounding against the eardrums. And in the glare of sunlight, Eagle was throwing a wide shadow across the ground.

Hope leaped through Sundance. The horse looked down at him out of large eyes. Sundance began the twisting and turning again, as much as the taut lashing allowed, hoping Eagle by some miracle might understand. Eagle pawed the ground, whinnied, but did not comprehend.

Sundance groaned. "I taught him everything else. Why in hell didn't I teach him to chew through rawhide?"

Lashed to the saddle was a bedroll and precious bags containing his Cheyenne weapons. But they were of no use to him unless they could be reached.

The more Sundance spoke to the horse, the more upset the animal became. Eagle pranced about trumpeting, then would halt and stare at Sundance in bewilderment, unable to understand why this Cheyenne master who had miraculously escaped so many previous traps seemed immobilized by this one.

Sundance knew he had to work fast; sand in his hour glass was not trickling but spilling fast. With the pain, the searing heat, his thinking began to be muddled once again.

Steeling himself against pain, he tried to attract Eagle's attention. "Teeth, teeth, teeth," he yelled, first in Cheyenne, then English, as if the horse could understand. Sundance felt foolish for even trying. The shouting upset Eagle even more. He reared back, forefeet pawing the air. Then he ran in a circle, head up, seemingly puzzled that Sundance, instead of lying in the hot sand, did not leap upon his back.

"*Goddam it!*" Sundance roared, the nibbling pain now spreading near the groin. He bucked and heaved and twisted and turned, all the while cursing the ants, Big Luke, and his own helplessness.

Suddenly, as every tendon in his body strained almost to the breaking point in his desperation, the movements of his upper body were more pronounced. At first he didn't realize it, thinking it to be hallucination because of the pain and brutal sun.

The stake to which his left wrist was bound had moved slightly. His bicep bulged as he strained. Sweat ran into his eyes and the greater arching of his frantic body actually spilled some of the ants.

Again the stake moved. He tugged, twisted his wrists, saw the piece of ironwood give minutely, then inch by inch from where it had been driven into looser sand than the other three. And then he was sitting up, the free hand sweeping aside the ants. He freed himself, leaped to his feet. He found a cleared sandy space and rolled about, dislodging those scurrying ants out of reach on his back.

Then he stood over the ant hill where he had been tied. He thought of trampling it. Then his thinking returned to its Cheyenne rationality. He never hunted unless hungry, never killed an animal unless threatened. Only a rattler would he kill, and then only because of possible future danger to a woman or unthinking child.

Kneeling at the waterhole, he dipped precious

fluid to ease the smarting at his belly. He washed off the honey. Then he stood up, facing the sun, head back, and from his lips burst a terrible Cheyenne war cry.

If Big Luke and the other three renegades were within earshot, which he doubted, they would know its meaning. They were doomed.

13

Big Luke had taken his Colt and rifle. It did not matter; this was Indian vengeance to be settled with Cheyenne weapons, not white man's. People of his own blood had left him to die by torture; they threatened to sell a white woman into slavery.

He took their trail.

As the hours passed, the trail was fresher. Sundance stayed back, keeping Eagle at a fast walk, which would not only diminish dust but also distance between slower-moving renegades and swifter pursuers.

Sundance's luck held until he came suddenly to a bend in a canyon he had been traversing for some distance. His calculations told him that his quarry should still be a mile ahead. Their dust which he had seen for the past hour, was now obscured by a lofty shoulder of rock. In his eagerness he had not considered this.

He came upon them abruptly, because Black

Moccasin's pony seemed lame. Black Moccasin dismounted and inspected the forefoot. His face was turned so that Sundance could see the profile of crushed nose, and lips that had been smashed against the front teeth.

Hunter was up ahead some ten yards or so, Lila sharing the pony. Evidently Big Luke had decided to give his own mount a rest by shifting Lila to Hunter's pony. She sat stiffly, only a two-fingered grip on Hunter's belt, as if disdaining even that much contact with the man.

Big Luke was swearing at the delay caused by Black Moccasin's pony. So far, none of them had spotted Sundance there by the rocks.

Two Trails, with the brand of slavery on his sweated forehead, looked on stoically, a war lance with its feathered tip resting across his thigh. He dismounted and, carrying his war lance, went to inspect the lame pony with Black Moccasin.

Crossed Arrows, mounted on a dun, held a carbine; its stock had once been splintered but was now held together by wrappings of rawhide. He rubbed his flat nose and laughed at something Two Trails shouted up at him in Apache. Big Luke didn't think it humorous.

Lila was rigid on the back of Hunter's horse, brushing strands of golden hair out of her eyes. It was when her head was turned that she saw Sundance creeping through the rocks of the narrow canyon on foot, throwing ax at his belt, bow and quiver of arrows on his back. He gripped his war lance and was prepared to hurl it at the nearest of the four dark bodies, Black Moccasin's. But just then Lila gasped and instantly clapped a hand to her lips to cut off the scream that Sundance's sudden appearance had sent surging into her throat.

In that moment her stifled gasp alerted Hunter, who looked around. His eyes flew wide. "Back from the dead, by God! Luke, *behind* you!"

Luke's followers were well-trained, Sundance had to give them credit for that. Without waiting for Luke's command, Crossed Arrows drubbed heels against his pony's flanks. And as the animal lunged forward, he aimed the carbine. Pivoting, Sundance escaped the wildly-charging horse as a jet of smoke burst from the carbine muzzle. A bullet clipped neatly through a few strands of his yellow hair. And as horse and rider drew abreast, Sundance's war lance was poised. Momentum of the hard-running pony drove the lance into the belly of its rider with such force that the point erupted through his back.

Lila's scream blended with the crash of the pistol Big Luke had drawn. In that instant Sundance recognized the weapon, and the thought spun through his mind that he never in his life had expected to be shot by his own Colt. But the shot, instead of hitting him, ripped an ironwood bush down canyon.

Hunter was yelling, "He can't be alone! Somebody cut him loose!"

Big Luke, realizing the possibility, knew that the narrow canyon was no place to maneuver a horse against the odds indicated by Hunter's shout. Luke flung himself to the ground near Black Moccasin, who had nearly been run down by Crossed Arrows' pony. The animal was now running free, its rider grasping the embedded war lance, as if in a futile dying effort to pull it from his body. He tumbled almost gracefully off the pony's rump.

Black Moccasin shouted obscenities and closed in

on Sundance with a spitting pistol, Big Luke forced to withhold his fire to keep from hitting his own man in the back. But Black Moccasin's shots quickly thumbed off. They hit only the canyon floor. Sundance, throwing hatchet in hand, did not relinquish his hold on the weapon, but held it as a man would a machette in the business of hacking brush. Its razor-sharp blade cleaved a wedge of skull near Black Moccasin's left ear, severing the faded red head band, slashing up into the crown of the head. Some of the spattering from the ghastly wound drenched Big Luke only a few feet behind him, and even as Black Moccasin was falling dead, he jumped back to escape more of it.

Two Trails hurled his war lance, missed, then made a desperate grab for the pistol Black Moccasin had dropped.

Sundance, trying to keep out of range of his own Colt in Luke's big fist, knew there was no way to prevent Two Trails from seizing the dropped pistol. He hurled the throwing ax. Instead of centering the chest, Two Trails moved and the blade sheared into the left arm. Two Trails screamed, spun around, and collapsed, leaving a raging Big Luke for the first time without cover.

On the run, Sundance had bow and nocked arrow in hand. Two of the bullets whipped past his head as Luke cursed his dodging figure. A third sliced through a fold in the right legging. Probably no more than fifteen seconds had elapsed, twenty at the most, since Hunter had yelled his warning.

Big Luke's final shot went skyward as the first of the arrows struck deep, its flint point crashing through the breast bone. The second buried itself in the throat at such depth that only the feathered tip was visible. Luke toppled soundlessly.

Hunter came to life and twisted on his horse to shove a hand against Lila's back. "I've got a gun on her, Sundance! Get your hands up or she's dead . . ."

Sundance laughed, the chilling sound causing Lila's face to lose even more color. "You've got no gun. Hunter, get off that horse, or I'll shoot you off."

He lifted the bow and Hunter, already a witness to the destruction such a weapon could wreak, lifted both hands, and slid from the pony's back. "I tried a bluff and it didn't work." He was breathing hard, sweating. But he quickly recovered his aplomb. Hunter said, "Well, thank God you got rid of those bastards. Should've been just you and me all along. Now it *is* just the two of us. To split the gold."

"Just the two of us," Sundance said through his teeth, feeling let down, now that the savage encounter was finished for the time being, at least. There was still Hunter. And El Tigre. And God knew who else.

Sundance knew that somewhere to the south were the Apaches. It was only a matter of time before they picked up their trail. Their only chance was to keep on the move.

Sundance made Hunter turn his back while he patted him for weapons, on the chance he might have sneaked one when Sundance was making sure of the dead. There was no weapon. He retrieved a Colt and Henry rifle from the dead Luke. He made a quick search for a hideout but found nothing. As he straightened up he noticed Lila was standing, rigid as a pole, her face beginning to come apart.

He sprang to her and gripped the shoulders. "Steady," he urged. "Don't give way now. It's all over."

But she seemed not to hear. She stared, white-faced, at the sprawled dead; Crossed Arrows, a war lance driven through the lower body, Big Luke on his back, two arrows deep in breastbone and throat. Black Moccasin in fetal position, part of the brain exposed where Sundance's war ax had shattered the protective casing of skull bone.

Two Trails had recovered consciousness, a dazed look in the eyes, face twisted in pain. Blood gushed from the upper arm that had been nearly severed by the throwing ax. Sundance's attention was centered on Lila. He considered Two Trails out of it from loss of blood.

Sundance gave Lila a reassuring pat on the shoulder. "You'll be all right now."

Then he retrieved his war lance and the two arrows. He leaned down and pulled the throwing ax from Two Trails' bicep.

"I'll bind up your arm so you won't bleed to death," Sundance said in a low voice. "Then you ride. I'm giving you your life, but you damn well don't deserve it."

Two Trails, expecting to be killed, looked at him in surprise.

Sundance turned to Lila. "Can you tear off a strip of petticoat? I need it for a bandage."

She watched in horror as he cleansed his arrows and the lance of the throwing ax in mesquite.

"My God, how can you calmly go about pulling arrows and that spear out of dead men. Then . . ."

"Because I may need those weapons," he said grimly. "To save your life. And mine!"

"How callous," she muttered, still in a state of shock.

"Lila, did you hear me about the petticoat?"

Hunter was now some distance from the bodies, where Sundance had ordered him to wait.

Something made Sundance glance at Hunter standing beside the pony he had been riding. He saw a faint surprise on Hunter's face, a shifting of eyebrows. Then the face was forcibly composed. Sundance had all the warning he needed. Sundance was holding the Henry rifle that he had been inspecting while talking to Lila, not trusting Luke's possible careless handling of such an important weapon.

Alerted, he spun around. Two Trails was dragging himself over the ground, the rawhide wrapped stock of a carbine against his cheek.

"Hold it!" Sundance shouted. A wild shot from the badly wounded man might hit Lila who still stood unmoving at Sundance's back.

Two Trails crawled another foot or so, the left arm drenched in blood, a sing-song Apache death chant on his lips.

"Cheyenne, you die!" he cried. He was too far away for Sundance to reach in one bound, and the renegade's finger was already beginning to press the trigger. Two Trails was on his knees, screaming his chant, when the Henry rifle exploded a shell at almost the same moment that the carbine spurted a burst of flame barely discernible in the sunlight. As Two Trails dropped face down, Sundance whirled to see if Lila might have been hit.

"I . . . I guess I'm all right now," she said shakily. "I know you've done what you had to do. It . . . it just seemed so gruesome. And you just gave that Indian a chance for his life. And in payment he tried to shoot you in the back."

Sundance looked at Hunter, who was holding tight the hackamore of his pony. "You saw that Apache coming at me. You didn't yell a warning."

Hunter shrugged. "I sensed you'd finish him, no matter what."

Sundance's smile was icy.

There wasn't time to bury the dead, even though Lila made a feeble protest at what she termed the inhuman treatment of the deceased.

He explained that as warriors they were already in the land of shadows. They died as they had lived—violently.

"Besides, we've lost too much time already," Sundance told her. "You ride Hunter's horse. It's used to white man's handling by now. Hunter, you ride one of the others."

"Yes, sir, *Colonel!*" He was almost jaunty as he turned to the roan Big Luke had been riding.

Sundance rode up beside him. "We're riding to the stage road," he said coldly.

Hunter looked surprised. "Hell, that's out of the way."

"You heard me," Sundance snapped.

He had made sure no weapons were hidden on any of the horses the renegades had been riding. He had searched Big Luke for hidden weapons. He hadn't bothered with the three dead Apaches. It was the first bad mistake he had made since signing the contract with Eloise Hunter.

14

Within the hour Sundance's worry about Lila was alleviated; she seemed to have regained her strength and poise, despite the terror she had endured. Had Sundance not been lucky enough to catch her captors in the rocky and narrow slot of a deep canyon, there would have been more bloodshed. Suddenly, standing on top of a mesa, he saw the stage road below, a plume of dust moving from west to east, and a stage coach.

He ordered Hunter in the lead to move at a faster pace. When they reached the road, the stage was still to the west of them. He told Lila what she must do. He gave her some gold pieces, which she was reluctant to accept.

"I want you to tell those stage passengers the story of how you and your father were mired in quicksand. Tell it as if it had just happened. You understand, Lila? They'll be sympathetic. Say that Hunter and I rescued you..."

Hunter laughed. "Hell, that coach'll never stop for you."

"If it doesn't, then we've got a twenty-mile ride to the stage stop," Sundance said bluntly.

Lila leaned close. "But I want to stay with you, Sundance."

"You're going back to Whipple Creek . . ." He noticed Hunter had left his pony and was strolling along the edge of the stage road, a little too nonchalantly, pretending interest in the mesa where they had been only minutes before. Sundance said, "Don't get behind me, Hunter."

"I was just stretching my legs . . ."

"You heard me. I don't want you at my *back*! You understand English?"

"No reason to lose your temper," he said with a shrug. But he walked back to his pony, where Sundance could keep an eye on him.

Lila whispered, "It's my destiny to be your woman, Sundance. I feel it deeply."

"It can't be."

"I went to pieces back there and I'm sorry. I won't again." Her smile trembled. "I'll be as strong as any Cheyenne squaw." Her face was streaked with dust and sweat, the eyes bloodshot. But she was still lovely, and he knew that in one sense she spoke the truth; Lila Corey would make a good squaw. But any chance for a normal life had ended that day north of Bent's Fort, when he had found his parents slaughtered.

"You've got friends in Whipple Creek . . . don't forget that Ralph you told me about. When I settle things, I'll visit you. You deserve a share of the gold more than some people I know." He was thinking of Eloise Hunter.

Lila argued, then pleaded. But Sundance was adamant. "I've got a chance to help the Indian. But it takes money . . . a ton of it."

In a low voice he told her of certain anonymous high-ranking Army officers, sickened not only by broken treaties but by corrupt politicians, who heartily endorsed his plan. Money accumulated from the hazardous jobs he undertook across the frontier was banked, to be used to sway certain Washington individuals into saving the Indian instead of exterminating him, which would happen, Sundance and those in league with him believed, if present policies continued.

"I admire what you're trying to do," Lila said fervently, "but I'll be willing to wait . . ."

"And grow old wondering if I'd ever come back? No." She started to protest again, but he shook his head. The stage coach was getting closer. He gave her instructions. She was to stand with him in the middle of the road so that driver and shotgun guard could see that she was a white woman. "I'll try and show them I mean no harm."

"Sundance, I'll never forget you. Never!" She flung her arms around his neck, which seemed to irritate Hunter.

"Great show of affection," he sneered. "What've you two been talking about, anyway?"

Sundance spoke of his plans for Lila.

"Hunter, you open your mouth or do one damn thing to ruin Lila's chances . . ." He let it hang there and stepped close to the man. "Think of a castrated bull and remember it's where my first bullet will be. They may hang me for it, but you'll take a damned long time in dying."

Hunter licked his lips but made no reply.

Sundance forced Hunter to stand to his left and a little ahead of him. He wanted one eye on him at all times. Lila stood at Sundance's right. As the coach approached, Sundance lifted his right hand in the frontier signal of peaceful intentions. He saw the driver of the six-horse team shout at the shotgun guard at his side who was leaning forward to stare open-mouthed at the trio blocking the road. A warrior. And a white woman and white man. What the hell!

Warily the driver brought the six-horse team to a halt. Two passengers, faces drained, leaned out the coach windows to see what had happened. The shotgun guard cradled his deadly weapon, indecision on his face.

Sundance shouted up at them. "This girl just lost her father. She needs help. We found her and brought her here." Then he added, "She has money for passage. Her home is Whipple Creek. Will you see that she gets there?"

Color was beginning to return to the driver's face. "Hop in, lady," he told Lila.

And as she did so reluctantly, with a pathetic backward glance at Sundance, the shotgun guard leaned down. He was mopping his plump red face with a bandanna. He said shakily, "When I first seen you, I figured sure as hell we was gonna get hit by 'Paches. Swear I like to soaked my britches. Then I seen your yaller hair."

The driver's whip cracked, the team lunged into their collars and they were rolling. Lila, teary-eyed, leaned out to wave at Sundance.

When the coach had been enveloped in its own dust, Hunter said, "You wasted a hell of a lot of time with that foolishness."

"It had to be done."

As they started riding away from the stage road, Hunter's voice held an edge of excitement. "Now we go for the gold." He gave Sundance a speculative sidelong glance. "More than enough for both of us." He waited for Sundance to reply. When he didn't, Hunter frowned. "We've been enemies. Now we're partners."

The jovial laugh that followed, Sundance supposed, was intended to show that the past was forgotten.

Sundance reminded him that it wasn't. "Don't forget my contract with your wife."

"Tear it up. It means nothing, anyway. She had no right to sign a contract without her husband's permission. As long as I'm alive, it isn't worth the ink you wasted on it."

"As long as you're alive," Sundance said softly, and Hunter gave him a sharp glance.

They rode for an hour without exchanging a word, climbing steadily. For a time Lila's pony kept up with them, then wandered away.

Finally Hunter began to discuss the hiding place of the gold they were nearing. He described a lookout point where a good view of the location of the cache could be had.

"I'll confide in you, Sundance, if you'll agree that we're partners," Hunter said, riding close so that their knees touched.

"Partners . . . to the end."

They were moving up a long draw choked with mesquite and giant cactus. Ahead loomed higher peaks half-hidden in darkening clouds.

"I'll tell you what El Tigre told me yesterday, Sundance," Hunter said, smearing a sleeve of the tattered shirt across his sweated brow. "Four guards were left to watch over the cache. But Many Wolves said he had enough good medicine so that nobody would dare steal the gold."

"Don't count on no guards being there," Sundance advised.

"If there are, we can pick them off from the lookout. You with your Colt . . . me with your rifle . . ."

Sundance said nothing.

"Say that El Tigre got worried about the gold, no matter what that loco medicine man told him, and sent a dozen guards there. Too many for us to handle." Hunter paused, then said, "We could still come out on top."

It was midafternoon, and they paused beside a water hole to rest the horses. "Tell me," Sundance said, watching him.

"We both know Hatch is in the territory," Hunter said. "Let's get him and some good men, kill the guards, and take the gold for ourselves."

Sundance appeared to ponder. The skin on his belly was puckered from the myriad ant bites. "We'd have to split the gold with Hatch and his friends," Sundance told him.

"We'll figure a way out of that," Hunter said with a laugh.

"Christ, you'd kill your own grandmother for a handful of pennies."

"It'd have to be more than pennies," Hunter said with a tense smile.

They started riding again and soon came within sight of a towering sandstone cliff. A short ride up through a tangle of brush and they reached its base. Up the face of the almost perpendicular spire

Sundance could see where steps had been hacked. Some ancient people, he supposed, had cut the steps and used the summit as a lookout post.

Sundance loosened the cinch of Eagle's saddle. Then, when Hunter was staring up at the summit some seventy feet almost straight up, he quickly unlashed one of his *parfleche* bags and reached deep inside for Hunter's black-handled knife Moon Star had placed there. Hiding the knife under his buckskin shirt, he said, "Let's make the climb. You go first."

Hunter turned and eyed the Colt at Sundance's belt, the Henry rifle in his hand. "Better let me have a gun. If there are guards at the cache, they might spot us and try to pick us off."

"You climb. I'll worry about the guards."

Hunter reddened, the arrogant lips twitched. But in a moment he got himself under control. He began to climb up the steps in the sandstone cliff. Despite their arduous earlier crossing of the desert, here in the mountains he seemed fresh. Sweat made blotches on the back of his soiled shirt. Sundance came quickly, not wanting Hunter to get too great a lead. Despite his abrasions and the ant bites, he kept pace. From time to time they paused for breath. On one of those pauses Sundance looked straight up, seeing that a few feet below the summit was a ledge two or three feet wide. It resembled the brim of a hat, the summit its crown.

At last they reached the summit, a sandstone cap thirty feet long and twenty feet wide. If a man lost his footing and slipped over the side, he could be saved by the ledge five feet below. If he missed the ledge, however, he would sail into space to meet death on the rocks seventy feet below.

"This promontory is shown on the map that Mexican gave me," Hunter was saying.

"Gave you the map? Killed him for it, you mean."

Hunter smiled, then shrugged. "I climbed up here a few times when I was hunting for the gold." He hurried across the summit, and on the far side dropped to hands and knees to cautiously approach the edge.

Sundance also went to the far side but kept his distance ln case Hunter had any ideas of diverting his attention and then trying to shove him over the edge. Sundance knelt down. Hunter, a few feet away, was pointing excitedly to a round-topped hill some forty feet below.

"The guards have gone," Hunter said, his voice shaking. "They've filled the shaft again. I had dug it out. It goes straight down . . . to a million dollars."

Hunter stood up and then his face tightened as he saw something to the southwest that caught his attention. Sundance had already seen them—moving specks—approaching on horseback. Apaches.

"El Tigre, sure as hell," Hunter muttered. "You speak their language, Sundance. You can argue him out of killing us. And you've got to admit I did show you the location of the gold. Did it quite willingly, I might add."

"As my prisoner, you showed me," Sundance retorted.

Hunter stared. "You've got a strange look in your eye, Cheyenne," he accused.

"I think we'll have an audience soon," Sundance said. He drew Hunter's knife from under the buckskin shirt, tossed it onto the sandstone cap of the cliff where it lay glittering in the sun.

"How'd you get your hands on my knife?" Hunter demanded.

"I had a friend at the Apache camp."

"Moon Star," Hunter sneered. "She ignored me. I suppose because you've got a trace of redman's blood she decided to give you favors."

"More blood than a trace. A full half. And she didn't offer favors. Not in the way you mean."

Hunter's laugh was harsh as he ran a thumb along the blade of his knife. "With cold steel we settle the matter of gold and glory and the rest of it?" Hunter said.

"What we settle, Mr. Hunter," Sundance said through his teeth, "is the matter of Eddie Strong, who'll never be a warrior, thanks to your knife."

Hunter's blood-shot eyes were incredulous. "You'd risk facing *me* knowing in your heart I'll cut you to ribbons? All because of a crippled kid?" He shook his head. "At least I fight for something worthwhile, like gold."

"I've told you, the Apaches will never let you have it."

"Some way, I'll outwit them," Hunter said confidently, the old arrogant grin back on his lips. Hunter mentioned Sundance's Colt and rifle, the rifle Sundance had placed on the sandstone at his feet. "When I'm beating you with the knife," Hunter said, "you can shoot me. Is that the idea?"

"I want no advantage over the likes of you. It'll be knives to the end."

Keeping one eye on Hunter, he carried his weapons to the ledge five feet below, then quickly returned to the summit.

Hunter was peering over the edge at the glistening bodies far below beginning to make the climb. "You don't seem too surprised to see our Apache friends," Hunter said with a faint laugh.

"They lost our sign a few times, but they never quit. It was easier when they figured we were heading for the gold."

"El Tigre's with them. I spotted the bastard."

"I know." Sundance cupped his hands and shouted down at the Apaches scaling the great stone cliff. "El Tigre, I avenge a Cheyenne boy Blood Knife foully crippled. And in so avenging, it will mean good medicine for your people!"

Hunter swore. "Speak English, damn it!"

Sundance translated, which brought a tight smile to Hunter's lips. "Misplaced confidence," he said arrogantly. "You'll never get off this mountain alive."

"You won't kill me," Sundance said. "Maybe El Tigre will put me to torture. It's a long gamble. But I'm willing to take it."

"And after I kill you, El Tigre will be willing to make some deal about the gold. He's a superstitious fool, as you well know. And I'll play on those superstitions."

Wanting no binding at arms in the coming lethal encounter, Sundance started to pull off his buckskin shirt. Hunter, waiting until the garment was over Sundance's eyes, suddenly lunged, his glittering blade aimed at the heart. But Sundance had anticipated the treacherous move. Dancing aside, he pulled the shirt off and whipped it across Hunter's face.

Hunter bared his teeth. "You're dead, Cheyenne, dead! And I'll prolong your agony as much as possible."

"It'll be hot here," Sundance said, standing with Bowie knife in his hand. "Pull off your shirt. I'll give you time."

"And cut my throat while I'm doing it?"

"You tried it with me. I won't with you."

"How goddam noble," Hunter sneered. "Thank you, I'll keep the shirt on."

"Whatever you want." They began to slowly circle.

"Glad you got away from the ant hill," Hunter said. "If it hadn't been for you, I'd have tricked El Tigre into letting me go free. Now I'll have my pleasure."

Hunter pretended to test the knife edge. He suddenly leaped. Had not Sundance whipped aside he would have been disemboweled by the vicious steel.

They circled again, parried with their blades, eyeing each other. Sweat ran into Hunter's eyes. Sundance saw what he thought was an opening but when he struck, Hunter had cleverly sidestepped the glinting Bowie. Hunter moved smoothly, confidently. Sundance could see why he had been able to kill the best knife fighters among the Apaches.

Sundance's Bowie clanged against the steel of Hunter's fighting knife with great force; it was nearly knocked from Hunter's grasp. An awareness of Sundance's ability began to be reflected in the pale eyes. Footing on the sandstone was poor. Bits of sand worked loose and under Sundance's moccasins became slick as glass. Hunter's heavy boots seemed more firmly anchored. The men circled, crashed together, each avoiding piercing steel by a hair.

From the ledge now, coppery faces stared at the

spectacle of death being enacted a few feet above. With them El Tigre stood, face impassive, arms folded, the jaw outthrust.

"I'll help make you the greatest chief of the Apaches!" Hunter shouted to El Tigre. "This Cheyenne's blood will be the greatest medicine for you and your people!"

Sundance did not waste precious breath on a boast, but began to move carefully on the slippery sandstone, first right, then left. When Hunter dropped into a crouch, Sundance did likewise, chin drawn in tight to protect the throat. But even then Hunter's whipping blade nearly nicked the jaw.

Sundance, trying to avoid a sudden thrust, lost his balance. He went to one knee. Hunter made a desperate attempt to finish it by driving the point of his blade into the open mouth and out the back of the neck. Sundance barely pulled his head aside in time. He heard a grunt of surprise from El Tigre and the watching Apaches.

Bounding to his feet, Sundance pressed the attack. For the first time in the furious encounter, Hunter began to show concern. His lips tightened and the taunting eyes lost their gleam of confidence. Hunter gave ground, his boots slipping on the sandstone. But he quickly recovered and in desperation tried to rip his blade in an upward arc into the groin. Sundance was able to dance out of reach. Still Hunter pressed. Great blotches of sweat began to darken Hunter's faded shirt. Steel clanged on steel as Hunter tried to get past the heavy hand guard of the Bowie and sever Sundance's fingers. But Sundance's blade ripped open the front of Hunter's shirt, the tip making a faint red line across the chest, drawing blood.

"We've put on enough show for El Tigre," Hunter panted. "Time to kill you, Cheyenne!"

And he put all his effort into trying. Their blades locked together, their tense sweating faces inches part.

"You had a boy beaten when you fought him with a knife," Sundance hissed, "but instead of backing off, you deliberately crippled him to show off for the crowd."

"I don't remember showing off," Hunter snarled as Sundance contemptuously used his left hand to thrust him aside so that their blades were unlocked.

"'Course you don't remember. It wasn't any more important to you than squashing a bug."

Mercilessly Sundance bored in. Hunter backed, a flicker of fear building in the eyes. The heavy Bowie clanged against the handguard of Hunter's knife, cutting a finger. Hunter leaped back. A second finger was cut so deeply that it seemed to hang by only a thread of skin. Hunter screamed in pain and desperation.

Hunter dropped his knife. Blood dripped from the deeply cut fingers of the right hand. But in the left was a derringer.

"Black Moccasin's derringer," Hunter said, despite his pain. "He wore it under his leggings. You didn't think to look there, you were so wrapped up in that female. I took it off his body."

Sundance came up on his toes, seeing the wicked snout of the .41 derringer pointed at his chest. But he flung himself flat as the derringer boomed above his head. Before Hunter could get set to fire the remaining bullet, Sundance, flat on the sandstone, struck out with his knife, its tip cutting deep into Hunter's shin bones.

An awesome cry of pain burst from Hunter. Bleeding badly, he tried to recover his balance and line the derringer for its second and final shot. It threw a delicate puff of smoke skyward, because Hunter's head was suddenly thrown back as he instinctively sought to avoid the slashing blade. He didn't move fast enough. His throat opened suddenly, spilling its bright blood down the upper body. Hunter dropped the derringer, which fell to the sandstone. With his nearly-severed finger dangling grotesquely, the light went out of his eyes even before he stepped back, back to the very edge of the cliff. And then, as the Apaches stared impassively, his body shot far out over the edge and he was quickly gone from sight.

"You will follow him to the rocks below, Cheyenne," El Tigre said coldly. "Seize him!"

Two Apaches scrambled up the steps, some five feet to the summit where Sundance stood. They warily eyed his dripping blade still gripped in the bronzed fist.

Sundance spoke to El Tigre. "I do not want to kill these blood brothers. But I will not allow them to seize me and hurl me over the edge."

"Then I will order my men to shoot you," El Tigre said.

"You have your great medicine now. Blood Knife is dead."

"So is Many Wolves. His heart gave out during the excitement of your escape."

"Then he is already in the land of shadows and can speak to you from there." Sundance swallowed in his dry throat. He saw the glittering eyes of the two Apaches hoping to hurl him over the edge. And the others now bringing up carbines and bows, arrows nocked. Sundance lifted his chin. "Listen well, El Tigre, to what Many Wolves is trying to say. I will interpret for him. He speaks of sacred gold . . . and the good that gold can do not only for Apaches but for all Indians. Hear me out, El Tigre."

This was the moment; either El Tigre could give the order to blow him to oblivion, or he could listen to him. After agonizing seconds, El Tigre lifted his hand. "Talk Cheyenne."

Sundance spoke of his plans, both his own and some of those high in the ranks of the pony soldiers.

"Money can perform this miracle," he finished. "Your sacred gold can buy lives and freedom instead of lying hidden in the side of a mountain."

A faint smile touched El Tigre's lips. He spoke in English. "You have bought your life, Cheyenne. No white man preacher ever spoke with more eloquence." Then the eyes hardened. "Some of the gold I will give you. The rest must remain in the mountain. Do I have your word that never in this lifetime will you reveal the hiding place of that gold?"

Sundance gave his sacred Cheyenne oath; there was none more binding.

Cyrus Grimholdt in his black suit came to stare out the window of his assay office. He was surprised to see Sundance ride up on Eagle, leading a pack horse laden with what might be a sack of flour.

Sundance dismounted and looked at Grimholdt in the doorway. "Got something to leave for Mrs. Hunter. How about your safe?"

"Why, of course." Grimholdt blinked through his glasses. "What is it, anyway?" He peered out at the pack horse.

"Some of the gold Hunter found. A lot of gold."

Grimholdt was worried. "Sheriff's out chasing horse thieves."

They walked into the assay office and Sundance felt a sudden sense of danger, but it was too late. He half turned as the gun barrel smashed down on the back of his head. A second man hit him, and he went down. Somehow he got the feeling that there were three or more men in Grimholdt's office.

Water splashed in his face and he opened his eyes. The first thing he saw were cold blue eyes and a red mustache. Hatch! The killer with the woman's name. Another man, heavyset and bearded, stood beside him, smiling.

Sundance knew there was another man behind him, a gun aimed at his back. He didn't have to turn to know he was there. The assayer stood facing the wall. His hands were trembling.

"They made me set you up," he said to Sundance.

Hatch, without turning, told him to shut his mouth.

Hatch said, "You walked right into it, half-breed. After all you been and done in your time, you walked right into a simple trap. Where's Hunter?"

"Dead. I killed him."

"*You* killed him! I don't believe it."

"Why don't you go back to that mountain and take a look for yourself. The Apaches will be glad to see you."

Hatch was looking at the sacks of gold Sundance had been given by El Tigre. "We don't figure on going back to the mountain. I'd purely like to get my hands on the rest of that Apache gold. I know we'd never get it, not with the cavalry out beating the bushes. No, we'll have to settle for what you brought back. Looks like an awful lot."

Hatch turned to Grimholdt. "How much would you figure, Assayer?"

"I didn't get a good look at it. It all depends. Perhaps fifty thousand, seventy-five. I would have to spill it out and inspect it for purity, and so on."

Hatch was smiling now, a thin and evil smile. "Not on your life, old man. Nobody touches my gold but me."

The black-bearded man spoke up with some anger in his voice. "You mean our gold, don't you, Hatch?"

"Sure, Ben. Share and share alike, only I get a bigger share because I knew where the gold would be."

"Just as long as I get paid," the bearded renegade said.

Hatch said, "You'll be paid."

"Me too," the voice behind Sundance said. It sounded like a young voice, not too bright.

"You too, Billy," Hatch agreed.

"That's good, Hatch," Ben's voice said. "You want me to kill him now?"

"Just the Assayer. Use your knife. We're going to teach this stinking half-breed a little lesson before we ride on. Walk him outside and put the rope on him. This yaller-haired Injun here has put everybody to an awful lot of trouble. Burke Hunter wasn't hardly any kind of a real friend. I just don't like the idea of Burke being killed by a sneaking half-breed. By the time we get through with him he's going to have more respect for his betters."

Outside, they stood Sundance under their guns

while they mounted up. He thought of whistling up Eagle to come a-running, but knew they would just kill the fine big horse. For now there was nothing he could do but take it. But if he lived through this, he swore . . .

The thickset man called Ben came out of the assay office wiping his skinning knife on an oily rag. "The old man went to sleep like a baby."

"Get mounted," Hatch said.

The thickset man eyed the sack of gold tied at the front of Hatch's saddle. "You want me to carry that for you, Hatch?"

"Drag the half-breed," Hatch ordered.

Sundance decided he might as well try to make a run for it. Better to be shot than dragged. After being dragged a man often came out of it with a broken spine. He tried to dive to one side, but Ben's pinto, spurred hard, caught him in the back and sent him sprawling in the dust. He tried to get up, but now the kid named Billy took his pony in close and knocked him down again. Now, Ben had a firm hold on the rope they had dropped around Sundance. He wrapped it around his saddle horn and turned his mount. Sundance went down again.

"Waltz him around some," Hatch called out, and Sundance was down in the street again, tasting his own blood. He struggled to his feet and Billy rode in close and kicked him in the face.

Now the rope was starting to pull. It pulled harder and Sundance began to slide. The street was thick with dust, so the dragging didn't hurt much at first. Ben was using a short rope on him, so there was no chance to get a grip in it and haul in the slack. He tried anyway, and found himself being dragged along on his toes. He felt the friction heat burning through the moccasins.

Then Ben let the rope go slack and Sundance was down on his chest again. He almost managed to get up again, but by then Ben had looped out a lot more rope and rode the extra rope out hard and tight, yanking it easily with one free hand.

"Drag him right out of town," Hatch yelled, whooping and slapping his thigh with his hat. "Let the whole town see what this Injun is made of. Word'll get around that he ain't so tough."

Sundance made one last desperate effort to get up. Ben tumbled him in the dust with hardly any effort.

The rope hummed, and now Sundance felt gravel ripping his hands as he tried to keep his body off the ground. It was no use. Hatch and his new-found friends must have roped and dragged more than one man in their time.

Ben worked like an expert. He jerked sideways with the rope and flipped Sundance over on his back. Dust boiled up, choking his throat, stinging his eyes, and then he was being dragged faster and faster as Ben spurred his pinto. The top-dust of the street was soft, but underneath there were rocks and old roots.

The bearded man kept the rope looped around the saddle-horn. As long as he kept it there Sundance had no chance of pulling him out of the saddle. With the rope tight on the horn, there wan't a thing Sundance could do but suffer. His body bumped over the rutted street. He cursed himself instead of the man who was dragging him to his death. Half-blind with dust, he saw the blue sky twisting crazily over his head. His buckskin shirt was burned through with friction from collar to belt. A sharp rock threatened to rip the spine out of his back. Then they were shooting at him just for the fun of it. He knew they didn't want to kill him. Not yet. But he hoped one of the bastards would get careless and finish him off.

When the rope started to slack, Sundance rolled over fast. Grinding his teeth, he choked back the pain. Ben was exhausted from the great fun he was having. He took off his hat and began to fan his face. Then, to let Sundance know who was running the show, he flipped him over on his back.

"This is more fun than dunkin' for apples," Ben said when Hatch and Billy rode up.

Sundance got back on his belly, and Ben was too tired to do any more fancy flipping. Dusty sweat caked with blood was beginning to cake over Sundance's eyes. Both eyes were bad, and one was worse than the other.

He managed to raise himself up on an elbow. Billy was feeling his oats and jumped his pony over Sundance's back, then wheeled the animal and went over him again. They laughed loud and long, and Sundance swore that if he ever got out of this . . .

Didn't look like there would be much chance of that.

With all that gold burning up in his mind, Hatch had to have a drink. He was feeling that good. He unlimbered a flat pint bottle and uncorked it with his teeth. Aiming at Sundance, he spat the cork at him. It hit him in the back. That by itself, he vowed, would buy Hatch his death, if somehow he managed to stay alive.

Lying where he was, his eyes just about closed, all

he could see was horses' legs kicking and stamping. For a minute he felt like giving up, ending it here and now, with a lot of dirty names thrown at them. One or another of them would draw and kill him. Then rage shot through his mind like a white flame, and he knew he would never give up while there was breath left in his body.

Hatch was saying, "You reckon the breed has learned his manners by now? I'd say he's a hard man to teach. Let's give him another little tour."

Sundance squinted with the good eye. They were out near the edge of town, and he heard a horse coming from where the street ended.

It was the lookout for the gang, and now he was talking to Hatch. "Riders coming this way," he said.

"How many?"

"Looks like six. Could be the sheriff and the posse on their way back."

Hatch said, "Let's ride. No point going up against the law for no reason. We got the gold."

He threw the bottle away and said, "Kill the half-breed, Ben. Come on, boys, let's make tracks."

Sundance heard the sound of horses being turned away from where he was.

Ben said to him, "You don't get off that easy, breed. Hold tight now and I'll get you where you're going in a hurry."

This time there was no time for Sundance to do anything. The rope jerked tight and the dragging started again. Hatch and Billy were out front, Ben with Sundance's dead weight holding him back. Sundance heard him yelling at his mount, and he knew this would be last chance he was likely to get until he was dying and Ben rounded on him and finished the job with a bullet.

Sundance knew the skinning knife was still in his leggings. That was the one thing they had missed when they stripped him of his Bowie, throwing hatchet, and Colt. That long-bladed work knife was the last chance he had to get out of this.

Ben yelled louder, raking the animal with his spurs, slapping it across the withers with his hat. The animal whinnied with fright and started to run faster. Sundance started to yell too, grabbing at the stretched-out rope, screaming with pain and screaming to scare Ben's horse even more than it was. Then Ben's horse reared up instead of going forward, its forelegs plunging wildly.

The rope began to slacken and Sundance got a tighter hold on it with his right hand while his other hand reached back and down to his leggings for the skinning knife.

His hand found the knife and he slashed at the rope. It gave way with a humming sound, and then he was free of it and rolling over and over on the trail. Staggering to his feet, he switched the knife to his right hand, rubbing at his eyes. He heard Ben turning his horse and coming back to finish him.

He could see the bulk of horse and rider coming toward him at a gallop. Ben was firing fast. Two bullets missed Sundance, the second one just by inches.

Still rubbing at his eyes, Sundance heard two more shots, felt the hot wind of their passing. Ben threw two more shots, but he was in a panic, and they missed. Then he rounded his horse to chase after the rest of the gang. But he did it too fast, and the frightened animal threw him.

With a yell, he hit the trail and came up cursing like a madman. He yelled, "Hatch, come back here!"

Knowing he was on his own, he turned to face Sundance, who was coming at him with the knife. He started to beg for his life, and when he saw that was no use he began a wild, lumbering rush that drove him right onto the point of the blade.

Sundance braced himself to take Ben's weight, allowing the big outlaw to impale himself on the blade. It drove straight into the outlaw's wide belly. Sundance was still holding the knife when they both went down with a crash. He pulled out the knife and, with Ben still begging for mercy, drove the knife through his heart.

Everything was going black when he heard the dying man's scream.

15

Sundance opened his eyes when one of the five cowhands fetched a bucket from the pump and poured it slowly over his face. The shock of the cold water made Sundance lunge to his feet. The four other riders held him back, and he lay back on the boardwalk, his entire body a mass of pain. The cowhand with the bucket held the edge of it to his mouth and let him drink. His mouth was full of sand, his eyes watery and red.

"Ain't you a sight now," the rider with the bucket said. "Who are you, *what* are you, and where in hell did you come from? Mind telling us what's going on here?"

He shook them off; then they tried to help him into the saloon. Behind the bar the barkeep looked scared. He wasn't about to argue about giving this half-breed a drink.

"They killed Mr. Grimholdt," he said excitedly. "I seen these three men going into the assay office.

They were in there quite a spell before this Injun rode. Mr. Grimholdt came out then, and they went in together. Well, sir, I was curious so I kept watch from over here. In a couple of minutes the three riders and the Injun came out. They had stripped him of his weapons. I could see that plain from over here. Then they commenced to throw a rope on him and drag him. I recognized one of the men. Hatch! Used to work out at the Hunter place."

"You sure the Assayer is dead?" one of the cowhands wanted to know."

"Dead as you like," the bartender said. "After they started dragging this Injun out of town, I went over to take a look. The one with the black beard was the last to come out. He's the one that done it. Cut Mr. Grimholdt's throat ear to ear."

One of the cowhands said, "Son of a bitch won't cut any more throats. This Injun just killed him."

Sundance drank another glass of whiskey and asked the bartender to give him some water for his eyes. The barkeep set out a pitcher and, tilting back his head, Sundance spilled water over his face.

"They knocked me on the head, stole my gold," he said. "It's legal gold, or I wouldn't be bringing it in to be assayed. I didn't kill Grimholdt. That's all there is to it, except my name is Jim Sundance. Thanks for bringing me in. Now I got to be going after them."

The bartender looked at him with awe. "*You're* Jim Sundance! You're known the whole country over. But you ain't fit to travel. You got to let a doctor look you over."

Sundance shook his head and set down his glass. "No doctor."

Not so steady on his feet, he went outside. Two of the cowhands had loaded the dead outlaw on his horse and brought him back to town. After they heard what he had done to the assayer, they just dumped him on the boardwalk in front of the sheriff's office. Sundance went after them to get his Bowie and his Colt. Ben had taken them from him in Grimholdt's office.

He put the knife in its sheath, the Colt in its holster, and he went to get his horse. The dead man was lying on his back. Before Sundance left, he spat in his bearded face. One down, he thought, two to go. He found his hatchet in the assay office.

And then, while the town came out to watch, he climbed stiffly into the saddle and rode slowly out of town. The bad eye still hurt like blazes, but it wasn't blind, and for that he was thankful for nothing. The wounds in his back were bleeding, and the sun brought out bitter sweat that stung like a thousand knives. But he kept going. No matter how long or how far he had to ride, he would find Hatch and the kid called Billy. When that time came they would wish they had never been born. He had risked his life, had killed men, to get that Apache gold, and he wasn't about to let it get away from him now.

He rode steadily, enduring the pain, until he was two or three miles out of town. There was no sign of the outlaws. When he reached a bridge that crossed a small river, he turned Eagle off the trail and rode upstream until he came to a shallow place by a grove of greasewood trees. It was time to see to his wounds, to gather his strength for the journey ahead. He didn't doubt that it would be a long journey, and a hard one.

Climbing down from the saddle, he unsaddled Eagle and allowed the big animal to water and graze. He had been through this before, and he didn't need any doctor to tend his wounds.

Grimacing with pain, he stripped off the torn shirt, the deerskin trousers. Then he waded into the stream and lay in the sandy shallows, with the cold water running over his battered body. He lay there for a long time, while the chill water washed away the dust and the blood. After a while the hurt began to leave his body. Then he went back to his war-bag and unwrapped a shirt and a pair of pants, but before he put them on he found a small jar of the ancient salve used by the Cheyenne to heal their wounds. There was buffalo grease in it, and other things, some of them thought to be poisonous by the white man.

He rubbed it slowly and carefully into his wounds, into his shoulders, buttocks, the backs of his legs. When that was done, he worked on his chest, already scarred by old knife and bullet wounds, his ordeal of initiation into Cheyenne warrior manhood.

While he was doing it, Eagle came over and looked at him curiously, whinnying softly. Sundance spoke to the great stallion that had served him so long and so faithfully.

"We'll get them, boy," he said.

He lay in the soft grass by the creek while the heat of the sun soaked the salve into his wounds. The sun was beginning to slide down toward the west when he finally stood up and began to dress. A great weariness came over him, but at least the pain that had racked his body earlier was now just a dull ache.

Soon it would be dark and he was too tired to go on. He needed food and sleep. In the morning he would start again on the vengeance trail. There was no hurry. He would find them. He promised himself that.

Just before first light he was up again, splashing water in his face by the creek, while a pot of coffee cooked on a small fire. He drank coffee and tore dried antelope meat with his strong teeth. He was still tired from the ordeal of the day before, but already strength was flowing back into his powerful body.

Now he was mounted again and heading north toward the Mason River. He knew this country fairly well, had been through here some years before. On the other side of the Mason, there was a collection of shacks they called Cartersburg, named after some near-white Indian scout who decided he wanted to settle down and become a respectable citizen. Other Indians and half-breeds, some ex-Army scouts, and some from the Indian Police, had followed him there. The town stood on land that had once been the tail end of a reservation. Now its status was unclear, but the Army didn't bother it because it was peaceful and sometimes the Indians and half-breeds who scratched out a living there provided useful information.

He felt sure that's where Hatch and Billy were headed, the lookout, too. Sundance hadn't gotten a clear look at the lookout, and it was always important to know all the men you were after. No matter, he would kill them all.

He heard the sound of the river before he got to it. The trail dipped and ran straight into a fringe of cottonwoods, and the river was beyond that.

Sundance had been fired on at too many river crossings to take this one, or any other, head on. There could always be a man with a long gun waiting on the other side.

Staying well back from the river, Sundance rode downstream for about four hundred yards. He walked the stallion easy, out of sight of the river, making no noise, looking for a place to cross. When he found it, he walked Eagle across.

On the other side, he headed upstream again. The trees provided plenty of good cover on that stretch of the river. He didn't figure he had much to worry about until he got back to the trail crossing.

A little way up from where he had forded the river, he saw a dead horse rolling and floating in deep water, snagged and held by the branches of a dead tree, under a high bank. One of the animal's forelegs had been broken and the white bone showed through. The bone was badly splintered, and when the dead animal moved with the current, he saw the bullet hole in its head.

It didn't look like the horses ridden by Hatch or Billy. That meant it could belong to the lookout. No way to tell. But if it was the lookout's horse, that meant one of the gang was afoot, and it wasn't likely the others would let him ride double.

An outlaw, on foot and desperate, would be waiting to bushwhack the first rider to come along.

When Sundance was less than two hundred feet from the river crossing, he lowered himself from the saddle, keeping Eagle on a steady rein. When he thought he was close enough, he left Eagle in the cover of some rocks after sliding the Henry rifle from its scabbard. He stayed in the shade of the cottonwoods as long as he could without crawling, but when the trees got spaced, he put himself on his belly, with the rifle lying flat across the crook of both elbows. The first patch of shale he crawled over made him wince with pain, but he kept on going.

The trail ran across the river, then through a

jumble of rocks, rocks choked with brush, the perfect place for an ambush. But still there wasn't any movement, any sound.

Staying low, Sundance inched off the flat rock where he was. Then he rested for a while. It was hot and quiet. Back in the shade of the trees, he moved to the right of the brush choked rocks. It took him a long time before he got all the way around. He raised his head and saw the bushwhacker lying on his belly, the rifle ready in his hands.

Sundance got set to kill his second man in two days.

The bushwhacker knew his sneaky business, had picked himself a good spot. From the river side there was nothing to shoot at but the upper part of his face, and that wouldn't be an easy shot.

Sundance's eyes still hurt, but the range was short. Sundance didn't know this man, couldn't say that he had ever seen him before, and yet his mind was bright with hatred. It would be pure pleasure to put him out of action with bullets, and then work on him with the big Bowie. He forced himself to be practical. He drew a bead on the man's head, what he could see of it. It bobbed about a lot, and he guessed the bushwhacker was nervous. Sundance blinked his reddened eyes and steadied the rifle. There was no use waiting for the outlaw to settle down. If he missed the first shot, it could mean a stand-off.

He lined up the sights again and waited until the head bobbed just the right way. When he got it just where he wanted it to be, he squeezed the trigger. The bushwhacker screamed and jumped and rolled over.

Not taking any chances, Sundance put two more bullets through his chest.

Looking at the dead man, Sundance felt satisfied. Two down, two to go. He had a feeling that it wouldn't be as easy as this from now on, especially with Hatch. But smooth or rough, it wouldn't be over until he counted up to four.

He looked through the dead man's pocket and didn't find anything but a big silver turnip of a watch. Inside the case there was a cracked photograph, trimmed to fit. The picture showed a thin ugly woman holding a thin ugly child with fair curls. He snapped it shut and put it back in the outlaw's pocket. There was no gold on the body.

The dead man's saddle and gear were close by, and he looked for gold but didn't find any.

He left the body for the buzzards and rode on.

The country he was passing through now was part of the old reservation. It was desolate without being wild, flat and grayish-brown, exactly the kind of worthless land the Government would give to the Indians. Nobody else wanted it, nobody else cared about it. The Army had jurisdiction over it and didn't bother with it one way or another.

He rode easy, sparing himself pain, and when he got close enough to see it, Cartersburg looked more like a white man's town than an Indian village. Not that it was much of a town. Just a straggle of log houses on both sides of the trail. Smoke from cook fires spiraled up into the air.

There was no way to sneak up on Cartersburg, or any Indian town full of yapping mongrels. In hard times the Indians ate the dogs. Other times, they kept them around, half-starved and vicious, howling and barking the minute a stranger came close.

Flat on his belly, Sundance watched Cartersburg from the top of a treeless hill. He saw an Indian woman dragging a big iron pot from one cabin to another, a pack of dogs yelping behind her. She put down the pot and threw a stick at the dogs.

The horse hitched in front of Carter's Trading Post looked like the one belonging to Billy. Sundance wondered where Hatch was. Gone ahead probably, leaving the kid behind with some crazy story. Anything was possible with Hatch, who had learned well from his onetime friend, Burke Hunter.

Sundance's eyes scanned the town for any sign of Hatch's horse. There was none. The only other mounts in town were a bunch of Indian ponies, small and wiry, in a corral at the far end of the town. Hatch's horse was a big dun gelding, a fine-looking, spirited animal.

Hatch was the man he wanted most, principally because of the stolen gold and the fact that he had ordered the roping and dragging. But it would be dangerous if he rode around the Indian town and left Billy on his back trail. That could be even what Hatch was counting on. There was no way to know, and a man didn't stay alive as he had by making guesses.

Then, too, there was the possibility that Hatch had hidden his horse in one of the cabins, and was waiting for Sundance to go into the trading post after Billy. Could even be—another possibility—that Hatch had passed out some of the gold to the dirt-poor Indians and half-breeds. Maybe all the men, or most of them anyway, were waiting with cocked rifles.

Waiting for him to ride in and get blasted clean out of the saddle. Sundance reminded himself that these people weren't just any Indians. There weren't Navajo sheepherders or Pima farmers. Most of them had served as Army scouts or Indian Police, and even the old ones knew how to shoot.

It was a chance he would have to take, this figuring that the Indians would stay neutral. Poor though they were, they had been town dwellers for a long time. Nobody was out to take their town, their land, and the Army let them alone.

The village dogs were already setting up a howl before he had ridden twenty yards from the top of the hill. Before he had ridden much farther than that, twenty or thirty men appeared in the doorways of the split-log cabins. Most of them were holding rifles, and they watched in silence as he approached.

An Indian taller than the others stepped out of the doorway of the trading post and motioned to one of the young men, who picked up a handful of stones and drove off the snarling dogs. Once the dogs were silenced, it was very quiet, just a hot, dry wind stirring up the dust in the street.

The tall Indian wore a blue trooper's tunic without insignia, and his brown wool trousers were stuffed into dusty cavalry boots. What interested Sundance was the bullet-studded gunbelt strapped around his waist.

Sundance walked his horse in carefully, making no quick moves. If it came to shooting down Indians, he wasn't going to be the one who started it. The tall Indian couldn't be anyone else but Rufus Carter, as he called him, head man in Cartersburg. When Sundance was close enough to talk, the tall Indian held up his hand.

Now that Sundance was up close, Rufus Carter hardly looked Indian at all. He could have passed for a light-skinned Mexican, except that Mexicans usually weren't that tall. Sundance had never seen

Carter before, but he knew something about the ex-scout. He knew that he was tough, proud, independent, determined to make a life for himself and his family, apart from the white man and the Indians who still lived in the old tribal way. That he was a half-breed, a mixed blood, didn't necessarily make him a friend of other half-breeds, especially a half-Cheyenne whose people lived so far to the north. But it didn't have to make him an enemy either. Sundance knew he would have to wait and see.

"That's close enough," Rufus Carter said in English. It was good English, with a stiff, formal mission schood sound to it. "Tell me what you are doing here."

There was no welcome in his voice, none in his eyes, and Sundance noticed that his hand didn't stray far from his holstered Army .45.

Sundance said he was looking for two white men who had robbed him of much hard-won gold. He didn't say anything about being roped and dragged. That would diminish him in Carter's eyes.

"You are Sundance," Carter stated before he said anything else.

"That's right," Sundance answered. "You are Rufus Carter. I have heard of you."

The tall half-breed bowed his head slightly, acknowledging the compliment.

"I want trouble with no one but the two white men who robbed me of my gold. There were two other white men, but now they are dead. Have you seen the other two whites?"

Carter said haughtily, "I know your work, Sundance, and my people here want no part of it. We have made a life here, poor though it may be, but it is a life. We have no quarrel with any man, white or

Indian. All we want to do is to live in peace. Everywhere you go you stir up the white man against the Indian. You cannot leave things as they are. If you know who I am, then you know I have served for many years as the white soldiers' scout. I have seen their armies, their new weapons, their Gatling guns. All you do is stir up the Indian so that he may be slaughtered."

Sundance wasn't there to argue politics. "About these two white men," he said. "I mean to find them."

"There will be no killing here," Carter said. "You have no right to be here. You are not one of our people. You have trespassed on our land. The Army would not like it if it found you here. Especially they would not like to find you."

"One of those men is here," Sundance said. "At least one of them is. That horse!"

Carter said, "I am ordering you to leave my town. You will not bring your white man's quarrel to my town."

"You turn that man out, then I'll leave. Any other way—it's no."

"You are the one who must leave."

"Then you'd better kill me, Carter. Then I'll be dead, and so will you. How do you want it to be?"

Raising his left hand, the ex-scout pointed at Sundance. "You are known to be a reckless, dangerous man, but I must warn you, I do not wear this pistol just to impress other men."

"They gave you money to turn me back, is that it?" Sundance asked. "Kill me if I didn't want to go. Maybe kill me anyway. You have enough men to do it. The man with the red hair and mustache, did he give you money?"

Rufus Carter's eyes wavered and Sundance knew he was on the right track. Knowing Hatch, it couldn't have been very much gold. "I want that man in the trading post," Sundance said. "You can kill me and I'll kill some of you while you're doing it. I don't want it that way. I'll give you ten times, twenty times what he paid you when I get my gold back."

"You do not have any gold now?"

"I told you. They robbed me. But I will get the gold back and I will pay you. On my honor as a Cheyenne warrior."

"I am ashamed," Rufus Carter said. His eyes didn't want to meet those of Sundance. "My people have been poor for so long. We try to trade fairly with the white man, but he cheats us. The Indians, the hostiles, would burn us out, kill us, even the women and children, if they could. Or sell them as slaves to the Mexicans. Only our rifles keep them away. But even now the ammunition is running low."

"You'll get all the ammunition you need, new rifles, too. I'll see to that," Sundance promised. It was a promise he meant to keep.

"The man you want is in there," Carter said, jerking his head toward the door of the trading post.

Rufus Carter stepped aside, and Sundance went in with his gun unholstered. He thought he could trust Carter, but you never knew about men when they were poor enough, desperate enough. When he got inside, he saw the kid named Billy asleep on the packed-dirt floor with his head against the makeshift bar. He didn't holster his own gun until he reached down and took the kid's single-action from its holster.

Rufus Carter was in the doorway behind Sundance. "You aren't going to kill him?"

"He's asleep, he's dead drunk," Sundance

answered. "I could wake him up, even give him some coffee. It still wouldn't be a fair match."

"That is the best kind," Carter said with cold Indian logic. "You promise us gold and I believe you. No, the boy has no gold. Yes, Sundance, we looked when the red-haired man rode on ahead." Rufus Carter gave a wintry smile. "Here in this town we go in the ways of peace and honesty, but all men must bend when the bellies of the children are growling for food. I believe your promise of the gold. Kill the boy while he sleeps. We will kill his horse and bury them deep together. It will be as if they never existed. If the white soldiers knew we killed a white man, even a robber, it would be the end of us."

Looking back at the kid, Sundance knew that Carter was speaking the truth. He had sworn to kill the kid, and there was nothing to stop him. He remembered how the kid had jumped his horse over him while he lay bleeding in the dust. The kid deserved killing, no doubt about that. And yet the mean little son of a bitch didn't look to be more than eighteen. Sundance didn't know why he didn't just draw his gun and put him away for good. A lot of people he didn't know might be saved a lot of grief if he did.

"No," he said to Carter, "I want you to rope him good, keep him in a secure place till I come back this way. Then I'll take him back to stand trial for murder. Maybe they'll let him off with twenty years, since he didn't do the actual murder. That's the best he can hope for. Here's his gun. Watch him good. He's a killer."

Sundance had turned away from the kid and was handing the gun to Carter when he sensed a movement behind him. He spun around with the kid's gun in his hand. The kid had a sneak gun out, a short-barreled, double-action Colt Lightning, and was getting set to shoot him in the back. The .38 went off and a slug took off the top of Rufus Carter's ear. Then Sundance drew and fired in one fluid motion, and the kid's head exploded like a rotten melon.

"Bury him and the horse," Sundance said before he went out to his horse. "You'll get the gold. I'll be back."

Holding a neckerchief to his head, ignoring the blood that soaked it, Rufus Carter walked with Sundance and waited until he was mounted on Eagle.

"The red-haired man, I don't know his name . . ."

"Hatch," Sundance said.

"He told the boy to wait here. He said he was going to Rankin, some days ride north of here, to trade the gold for greenbacks. The boy was wanted up there on a murder charge as well as horse-stealing. This Hatch didn't want him riding along, he said. He told the boy to wait here till he got back, then they would ride south to Mexico and have a good time. He said they might even go partners in a big horse ranch. He left just enough nuggets to make the boy trust him, make him feel important. Spending money, he said."

"I'll be back," Sundance said. "Things will get better when you have the gold and new rifles."

Sundance was about to set Eagle to a canter when Rufus Carter told him to wait a minute. The ex-scout looked at him gravely. "Do not be too sure that Hatch is the last men you have to kill to get the gold back." Carter smiled. "You see, now I have an interest in the gold. I do not want you to get killed before you can help my people. Hatch has a way of getting people to follow him, and it is not only because of the gold. I have been told that people like the man for himself, murderer or not."

"You mean he'll be looking for more recruits?"

"You saw how he left the boy here to be killed. The boy served no other purpose than to delay you. That is what he did. I would say there will be others. Watch for two men who run a drinking place on the trail to Rankin City. You will pass the house on the way. Their names are Riggs and Burmann. I would not leave them behind me."

"How far?" Sundance asked.

"This trail leaves the reservation boundary about ten miles from here. Then it turns north and east. Riggs and Burmann have their place five miles from a big high rock with the white-washed words JESUS SAVES on the side of it. Some missionary put it there many years ago. Watch yourself, my friend."

"Thank you, my brother," Sundance said.

He touched his heels to Eagle's flanks and rode out of Cartersburg.

16

Ten miles from Cartersburg, Sundance dismounted, spilled water into his hat, and let Eagle drink. Then he ate some jerked antelope meat and drank himself. The country was still flat, grayish-brown in color, but up ahead he saw there was a range of low hills that rippled into the distance.

As Rufus Carter had said, the trail now began to turn east. Less than a mile from where he stopped, he saw the big rock with the faded sign. He looked at it as he rode past, thinking it was just like a missionary to paint a sign like that right in the middle of country that looked like the far end of hell.

Not long after that, Sundance was off the reservation and riding into the hills. The country was broken now, dotted with trees and rocks and ravines, good cover for ambushers, so he traveled carefully, watching both sides of the trail.

But nobody shot at him, and in less than an hour he reined in Eagle when he saw an unpainted frame building up ahead. It looked out of place in the bleak countryside, as if it had once been part of a town—and now the rest of the town had disappeared.

Remembering what Carter had said about Riggs and Burmann, he left the trail and rode out wide, taking Eagle down into a deep ravine that ran parallel to the road. The ravine ran past the frame house, then sloped up again about a hundred yards from there. Then watching carefully, he rode Eagle back onto the road, crossed it quickly, and began to head for the back of the house. On the far side of the road the ground was rocky, and he walked Eagle the rest of the way, so as not to make any sound.

At one end of the house there was a lean-to with two horses feeding at a hay rack. Neither of the animals looked like Hatch's horse. He looked for a sign that had the names Riggs and Burmann on it. There was a sign, but the name on it was Hazen's Way Station.

The two horses in the shed whinnied when they smelled Eagle. There was nothing Sundance could do about that. He left Eagle at the back of the shed and edged around the side of the building. Just then a thin, lanky man in a leather vest and a flat-crowned hat came out onto the porch and looked down the south trail, the one Sundance had just traveled. He looked long and hard, as if expecting somebody to come from that direction.

"Damn horses," he said, before turning to look up the north trail. "Don't see anybody coming," he said to someone inside the house. "Not a soul in sight."

Sundance, flat against the side wall of the house, didn't move until the man went back inside. Now, inching along the front porch, soft and rotting in spots, he reached the door and heard two men talking.

"Maybe he won't come," one said. The voice sounded foreign, maybe German. That could be Burmann. A man with a name like Riggs wouldn't be likely to have a Dutch accent.

"He'll be along," the other voice said confidently. "You can count on that. And that's for damn sure."

"Maybe he can't travel. After what happened to him, is what I mean."

"He'll come."

"I ain't that eager that he should. Money is one thing, but . . ."

Sundance stepped through the open door, and found himself in a big cluttered room that looked like a combination saloon and general store. On one side was a bar, wide planks laid on cast-iron trestles; on the other a counter and shelves that went from floor to ceiling. On the shelves were rows of boxes and canned goods. One of the men was behind the bar, the other in front of it. A bottle and glasses stood between them.

They turned quickly when Sundance came in, noiseless on moccasined feet.

"What in hell!" the man with the Dutch accent said. Neither of them made any move toward their guns. Sundance didn't have a gun in his hand, but his hand wasn't far from it.

"You surprised us, mister, coming in so soft," Riggs said. His hard gray eyes took in Sundance's get-up. They didn't miss the deadly straight-handled throwing hatchet slung from his belt. Riggs' eyes managed to be hard and shifty at the same time.

"Something we can do for you?" Burmann asked, displaying gold teeth when he smiled. Burmann didn't look like any kind of gunman. Sundance knew that didn't mean anything. People always said that Wyatt Earp always looked like a farmer come to town for a church social.

"That's right," Riggs said. Burmann didn't come out from behind the bar, and Riggs stayed where he was. "You want whiskey, supplies?"

"Whiskey first," Sundance said, moving over to the bar.

Keeping his hand away from his gun, Burmann reached back and found another glass. He set it down and placed both hands on the bar.

Sundance poured his drink with the left hand and let some of the whiskey trickle down his throat. It was very bad whiskey, even for a place like this. The way station, so called, was thick with dust and had a musty, rundown smell.

Riggs was inclined to be chatty. "Not often we get travelers up this way. Business, as you can see for yourself, ain't exactly booming. Bought the place when it looked like they were going to open up that old reservation. Hazen, the original owner, had the same idea. Expected this trail would be sort of a main road, all kinds of travelers passing by. Not so."

Sundance, the glass still in his hand, said, "I'm looking for a man named Hatch. Red hair, mustache the same color, early thirties. Riding a dun gelding."

Burmann exchanged glances with his shifty-eyed partner. "What would you be wanting him for, mister?"

Sundance said, "Hatch and three men robbed me. Took a sack of gold I was taking to the assay office."

"A sack!" Riggs said. "That sounds like a heap of gold. Dust or nuggets?"

"Nuggets. Can't be sure how much in money.

Didn't have time to get an assay. The Assayer guessed between fifty and seventy-five thousand. Could be even more."

Burmann whistled. "Jesus! That's some sack of gold all right."

"I'll say it is," Riggs said, again trading glances with his partner. They didn't look too happy.

It was plain to Sundance that Hatch had lied to them too. Probably paid them fifty dollars apiece to protect his back trail. He had shortchanged them just as he had double-crossed the kid.

He was waiting for them to make their move, but it didn't come, and he guessed they weren't that anxious to take him on, now that they knew they had been crossed. He was looking at Riggs when it came to him that he looked a lot like the kid he had downed back in Cartersburg. His brother?

"You know this Hatch?" he asked them.

They were too quick to answer. They both answered together, "Never heard of him."

Sundance realized that he would have to force a fight on them. It was the only way. He didn't want to have to tangle with them later. If he rode out, they'd be riding after him, dogging his trail, waiting for him to lead them to Hatch. They would wait until he had the gold, then try to kill him in an ambush.

Sundance, steeling himself for the killing to come, had another drink of whiskey. "Hatch used to have a gang," he said. "There was the big man called Ben. I put a knife in him back on the trail. Gutted him like a pig." Sundance sipped his drink. "Later on there was a banty little killer that tried to bushwhack me at the river crossing. He's still there with three bullets in him. Got around behind him and killed him where he lay."

Burmann's heavy red face remained impassive, but Sundance saw the tension building in the other man's eyes. Now he was sure he wasn't mistaken in the resemblance he saw between Riggs and the kid called Billy.

Riggs, his shifty eyes narrow, set down his glass and rested his right hand on the edge of the bar. Sundance went on.

"Then there was the third man, more a kid than a man. Looked like a half-wit degenerate more than anything else. A kid like that would have a whore for a mother."

Burmann knew what was coming, and he tried desperately to head it off. "So much gold was stolen," he said, his way of trying to remind his partner of all the money at stake. "The man who finally gets that gold will be a rich man."

Burmann's eyes were desperate, but Riggs didn't seem to hear him. The knuckles of his right hand showed white. "This kid you're talking about," he said in a strained voice. "What happened to him?"

"I killed him in his sleep," Sundance said.

"You stinking, murdering savage!" Riggs screamed as his hand streaked for his gun.

He was fast. Faster than Sundance expected him to be. It didn't make any difference. Riggs' gun had cleared the top of his holster, the hammer going back, the cylinder turning, when Sundance's Colt boomed twice. Burmann was still going for his gun when Sundance turned the Colt on him and blew a hole in his head. The impact of the heavy bullet sent him crashing back against the row of bottles behind the bar. He slid to the floor. Riggs had dropped his gun and was on his knees, trying to pick it up, but his hand had still a long way to go before another slug struck him squarely in the face under the left eye. He went over backward and lay still.

Sundance opened the loading gate of the Colt and poked out the empty shells. Then he reloaded.

Five men were dead—and Hatch was still out there with his gold.

Before he left he helped himself to a can of coffee and a thick slab of bacon. He mounted up, heading north again toward Rankin City. It was said to be a wild town, and maybe Hatch had plenty of friends there, and if he hadn't—there was enough gold to buy all he needed.

Before he left the way station, he searched for a shotgun that could be shortened into a scattergun. It was a weapon he hardly ever used. Now he had a feeling he was going to need it.

Two hours travel from the way station, he saw a house off in the distance. It was a frame house painted white, and it had two stories. Cottonwoods grew in close, putting the house in shadow. There was a windmill, one of the new ones with steel blades, turning listlessly in the hot dry air. The windmill made a creaking, lonesome sound.

The place looked deserted. There was no sign of livestock, not even a dog to come out yapping. Some distance from the house was a big Swedish barn, red-leaded but not recently. The barn had a huge black cross painted on the side of it. There was lettering that Sundance took to be German or Scandinavian. He thought of the JESUS SAVES sign he had passed back on the trail.

Close to the house there were two graves. One was grassed over and looked like it had been there for years. This grave had a headstone made of sandstone, which was flaking away in the sun. The other grave was recent, the dirt still piled high. No gravestone here, just two lengths of white-painted wood, crossed and held together with a single nail. The second grave looked no more than a few months old.

A door banged and a girl came out. Her skin was a light golden brown, fair skin tanned by sun and wind. She looked up at Sundance and said, "Welcome, stranger." She had a slight Scandinavian accent and she put a V instead of a W into 'Welcome.'

"You here all by yourself?" Sundance asked.

"I'm used to it," she said. She didn't seem to find anything strange about his appearance. Her hair was the same color as his own. "My name is Helle Lindberg. Do you want to come in for a while? There isn't much food, but I can find something."

"At least there's coffee," Sundance said. He got down and gave her the can he had taken from the way station. "My name is Jim Sundance. There's bacon to go with the coffee."

There was time enough to ask her if she had seen Hatch passing this way. He didn't quite know what to make of her. A woman alone was prey for every straggler and saddlebum, and yet she didn't appear to be afraid.

Looking at the two graves, he asked, "Your folks dead?"

"My mother for a long time, my father three months ago. He was a farmer and a preacher. A good man but very strict with me. Any young man who would come to see me he would chase away with a shotgun."

A shotgun, Sundance thought.

"I'm sorry about your folks," he said, adding, "My folks are dead too."

"Then you are alone as I am."

"I guess so." Sundance, in all his years on the move, had never thought of it like that.

They went into the house, and while the coffee was on the stove she sliced the bacon and laid the strips in a skillet. After the jerked antelope meat, Sundance was ready to eat a real meal.

"I have canned peaches for dessert," the girl said.

In a while there were two plates of fried slab bacon in front of them. They both ate hungrily, enjoying the smell and the taste of good fresh coffee.

After they finished the canned peaches, Sundance looked at her across the table. "Maybe it's none of my business, but how do you manage to live?"

"I sell my body to men who pass by on the road," she said, her eyes steady and without shame. "Out here there is nothing else I can do. I have never been away from here, not even for a single day, in all my life."

"You could sell the place, take the money, and move to some town."

"What would I do in some town? This is where I have always lived. Anyway, I would not get much money for this place. Nobody wants to live here. The land is no good, the soil is all blown away by the wind. In a few years it will be nothing but dust. Some man wanted to tear the barn down and build it up again some place else. I said I would have to think about that."

The girl seemed lost, and Sundance didn't think there was much anybody could do for her.

"Did a man with red hair and a red mustache stop by here?" he asked, finally getting down to it. "Tall, in his early thirties. On a dun horse."

She looked surprised. "Your voice is very cold when you speak of him. What did he do to you?"

Sundance just told about the gold, nothing about the killings.

But she seemed to know. "You are going to kill him. That is strange because he is such a pleasant man. He stopped to fill his canteens. He smiled at me and said I was a pretty girl and ought to get married and move away from here. He gave me a dollar for filling his canteens. I asked him if he wanted to go upstairs with me. He smiled and said he would like to, but was in a hurry. Imagine! A dollar for two canteens of water."

Sure, Sundance thought sourly, everybody liked red-headed Bev Hatch, the killer with the woman's name.

"Did he really steal your gold?" the girl asked. "Perhaps it was someone else."

Sundance, wanting to get on with it, asked her if he could buy her father's shotgun. "You mentioned he had one. Is it still here? I will give you a good price."

"To kill this man?"

"For protection," Sundance lied. "All I want is my gold back."

"If I give you the shotgun, you must promise not to kill this man. He was nice to me, and I do not want to see him killed."

Sundance wasn't going to make that kind of promise. "We'll see what happens," he said. "The shotgun, I'd like to look at it if it's still around."

"It's around," she said, not too sure that it was. "Upstairs, I think. Come with me."

Sundance followed her down a narrow hall. The upstairs of the house was low-roofed, and he had to duck going through the doorway. There was a big wood-framed bed with an elaborate head-board.

The bed was painted white, like the pine dresser set against the wall. The top of the dresser was ringed with bottle marks and scarred with cigarette burns.

Up there under the roof, the little sleeping room was hot and stuffy. The faded patchwork quilt that covered the bed was singed and holed with cigarette burns. The room smelled of stale liquor and sweat.

To one side of the bed there was a narrow closet. She opened it and took out a package wrapped in oil-skin. She handed it to Sundance. He opened it and found a double-barreled, English made shotgun, a Smithers. He snapped open the breech and it was unloaded.

Downstairs in the kitchen, he looked through the barrels. They were clean except for a thin film of dust. "You got any shells for this?" he asked her.

"In the drawer over there. My father shot our food with that gun. There is plenty of ammunition."

Next Sundance asked her where her father kept his tools. "Out in the barn. Hammers, saw, chisels, things like that."

What Sundance hoped to find was a hacksaw. Without a hacksaw there was nothing he could do to shorten the twin barrels of the 10-gauge. Shortening the barrels would turn a good hunting gun into one of the deadliest weapons in the world.

She followed him out to the barn and watched while he went through the dead preacher's toolbox. In the bottom of it he found a hacksaw in a frame, rusted but still sharp. He took the 10-gauge over to the vice at the carpenter's bench and clamped it in as tightly as he could.

He measured off eighteen inches from the twin hammers toward the muzzle. Then he marked the place he had to saw with a blue carpenter's pencil.

It took him less than five minutes to saw through the twin barrels, and when he was finished, he got a small file and smoothed down the jagged edges. Then he cleaned and oiled the scattergun, as it was now, and went back to the kitchen to get two boxes of cartridges. If he didn't get the job done with two, he wouldn't get it done at all.

"Would five dollars be too much to ask?" the girl asked him when he was getting ready to leave.

Sundance had about fifty dollars in bills, and he gave her most of it.

"Take care of yourself," he said, looking down at the girl. He didn't think she would. Sooner or later some drunken renegade would ride in and . . .

"Maybe next time you come you'll have time to go upstairs with me," she called out as he rode away.

17

Sundance made good time without pushing Eagle too hard. If nothing happened to slow him down, he expected to reach Rankin City in two or three days. Hatch was headed that way, he felt sure, and if not there, then some other town. He'd find him.

He was down on the plains now, heading straight north. About twenty miles ahead there was more hill country, and beyond that another stretch of flatlands. It looked like Hatch was making good time, too, stopping only to rest his mount for a few hours, and then pushing on as fast as he could. Sundance wondered how far Hatch could travel before his horse started to give out.

It was getting close to nightfall on the second day when the trail began to climb upward again. Sundance followed it into the hills. The trail narrowed as the hills, scattered with rocks and brush, closed in on both sides. Most of the ache in his long, lean body was gone now. He kept going.

Darkness was coming down fast, but he decided to give it a few more hours. There was no moon yet, and the hills crowding down on both sides darkened the trail even more. When Eagle stumbled and nearly fell, he climbed down and walked on ahead, holding the reins. It was a hard trail to ride, any way you looked at it, and it was that much worse at night.

Something moved off to the right, and Sundance's gun came out, the hammer cocked. The dry click of the hammer going back seemed to make a lot of noise in the dark silence of the hills. There was another scraping sound and the thorn bushes rattled. Sundance stopped and waited.

It was moving slowly, whatever it was. Probably some night-hunting animal, or a big diamond back out to kill a rabbit. Or it could be a man dragging a piece of deadwood on the end of a long rope, exactly the kind of trick a bushwhacker like Hatch would know.

Now it was moving down the slope, coming his way. Sundance put away his gun when he heard the funny snuffling sound. Most Indians and some white men could do a fair to middling take-off on a coyote or an owl, but nothing but a real night-prowling badger could make a sound like that.

He moved on. The moon was trying to break loose from behind the black, rolling clouds, and he hoped it would come out just enough to make traveling easier. But he didn't want to be a slow-moving target, with the moon lighting every step of the way.

At the rate he was going, it would be close to morning when he got clear of the hills. He meant to ride down the far slope come morning.

The clouds cleared suddenly, and the moon lit up

the hills, washing them in a white glare. After the darkness, Sundance felt as if he were standing in front of the headlight of a locomotive. He decided to keep moving, moon or no moon.

A mile up ahead the hills fell away sharply, and the trail dipped into a long, shallow basin, floored with sand and grown over with brush. It was about six hundred yards to the other end, where the hills closed in again and the trail grew narrow and rocky again.

The clouds rolled in again, darkening the moon but not dimming it completely, and a long way over in the shadows there was a wild squawk and a frantic flutter of wings as a bobcat went after the eggs of a ground-nesting bird.

A hundred yards past that there was no noise except for the chirping of crickets. Then the crickets stopped and oily black clouds rolled over the moon.

Sundance climbed down and waited for the crickets to start up again. He could barely see the dull shine of the shotgun in his hands.

The shotgun felt solid and heavy, its twin barrels charged with death. Eagle whinnied softly when Sundance turned him loose. The big stallion stayed close to the trail, kept there by the thorny brush.

Sundance walked for some distance until the thorn bushes began to thin out, then he moved off the trail, gritting his teeth as the thorns ripped at his already lacerated body.

Suddenly a rifle opened fire from darkness. There was only one shooter, it looked like, but he was shooting and jacking shells as fast as he could pull the trigger and work the lever. The muzzle flashes split the darkness and the explosions ran together like a drum roll.

Sundance yelled like a man hit bad. The fire

slackened and stopped and he could hear Eagle's frightened whinny in the darkness. Sundance started to move in closer, moving through the sandy basin like a ghost.

He looked up at the night sky. It was darker than before, and wasn't about to break. Over in the bushes, to the left, he heard movement and loosed one barrel of the shotgun. The heavy cartridge exploded like a small cannon, the noise rolling and echoing far back into the hills. There was another movement in the brush, a little farther away now, and Sundance let loose another blast.

The rifle cut loose again, and in back of him Sundance heard Eagle scream with pain and fright. He turned but couldn't even see the outline of the big horse. The sound made the hair stand up on the back of his neck. After all the years they had been together, in good times and bad! To have it end like this!

Suddenly it was quiet. Flat on his belly in the sand, Sundance thumbed two fresh loads into the 10-gauge. He guessed Hatch, or whoever it was, was down on his belly too. The next two shotgun blasts would have to be aimed low.

He rooted in the sand until he found a stone. It was still quiet. He pitched the stone toward where the ambusher was. It rattled through the brush, but no rifle bullets tore after it.

Sundance raised himself and fired off one barrel of the shotgun, but the rifleman didn't answer his fire. He rolled over in the soft sand without making any noise. The rifleman out there in the darkness was still holding his fire. Sundance wanted to get this over with. He wanted to get back and see to his horse.

Then Hatch's voice came from the solid darkness

of the basin. Sundance fired the other barrel, and was rolling again before the rifle jetted fire again. Four bullets thunked into the sand where he had been a moment before.

Sundance snapped open the breech and loaded again. A bullet snipped through the branch of a thorn bush not far from his head.

"Can't you take a joke, Sundance?" Hatch called out from the darkness. Sundance held his fire. "If I wanted to kill you, I could have done it in the assay office. Ben got carried away, is all. I guess you got all the boys, else you wouldn't be here, shooting at me. Only I ain't all the boys. Killing me won't come that easy. Look, what happened back there was a mistake. I was mad and kind of drunk. What's the difference? You're still alive, and there's more than enough gold for both of us. I don't want you dogging me till Doomsday. Why don't we make a deal? Fifty-fifty. What do you say?"

Sundance didn't say anything.

Hatch yelled, "You can shoot at me all night, won't do you any good. I'm in the only patch of rocks in this basin. Fire that scattergun all you like. Comes morning, won't be any different. I got cover, you got none. Any way you come at me, I got cover. All the water I need. What about the deal?"

Sundance fired the shotgun again, to see what effect the blast would have. There was none, and he figured Hatch was telling the truth about the patch of rocks.

He rolled again, going back the way he had come. Instead of firing back, Hatch yelled again, "Take the deal, Sundance. It's as good a deal as you can get. Don't take it and you get nothing but a bullet. What'll happen to your Injuns then? What do you say we wait till first light, no chance then of sneaking up, one on the other. We split the gold then. You go your way, or maybe we could team up."

Sundance wanted to spit, but he didn't do anything, say anything.

Hatch was at it again. "Your horse is shot. I didn't mean to shoot the animal. A fine animal. You can buy one just as good with your half of the gold."

Already, Sundance was edging back into the darkness, away from Hatch's voice, back to where Eagle was wounded—or dead. He crawled away silently, with Hatch's voice following him into the darkness.

The moon was still buried behind the clouds, and soon he was far enough away to disregard anything but a chance bullet. No one came his way and now he stood up, still protected by darkness, and still moving he found Eagle lying on his side, blood pouring from a wound in his neck.

Sundance whispered softly to the big stallion, and touched its neck. His hand came away slick with blood. Eagle whinnied softly with pain, and Sundance quieted the animal with a word.

"You'll be all right, boy," he said, wishing he could be sure of that. "Come on now, get up."

The big stallion raised itself to its feet, sweating and shuddering. Sundance clenched his fists around the stock and the barrel of the shotgun. This, the shooting of his horse, was one more thing he owed Hatch.

He stood in the darkness, holding the reins, whispering softly to Eagle, waiting for Hatch to start showering him with bullets again. But nothing happened, and he stood there for minutes, and still nothing came at him from the patch of rocks. Then he heard a wild yell and hoofbeats going the other way. North toward Rankin City.

Sundance, rigid with hate, waited for another five minutes. The hoofbeats going north had died away. There was always a chance that Hatch would come back. He didn't think so. No matter: he had to make a fire and look after Eagle before the animal bled to death.

As he gathered deadwood in the darkness, feeling for it rather than seeing it, he knew he was risking his life for a horse. If Hatch sneaked back, he could shoot him down in the light of the fire. But Sundance knew this was no ordinary horse he was risking his life for. Hardly that. Hardly that at all. Eagle had served him in the deep snows of Montana winter, in the bleached hell of the Sonora desert.

He heaped branches and deadwood together in a pile and touched a wood match to it. The bone-dry wood flared up instantly, its light throwing shadows across the shallow basin. He was able to see now, and he found more wood and piled it on. This could be no small Indian fire. He had to be able to see how badly Eagle was wounded, and if anything could be done.

The fire burned brightly and Eagle, though in pain, stood patiently until Sundance made a short motion with his hand, and the stallion rolled down on its side, holding its injured neck away from the ground. Sundance, kneeling beside Eagle, spoke softly, holding the skinning knife in his hand.

"This is going to hurt, boy," he said. He had felt the other side of the stallion's neck, and the bullet hadn't come through. It would have to come out, or blood poisoning would set in. He began to probe with the thin-bladed knife and the animal screamed with pain, its hoofs flailing. He spoke sharply to the horse and probed again with the knife, and this time the tip of the knife scraped against the lead slug.

Sitting on the side of the stallion, he felt the sweat coursing down its powerful frame. He knew it would have to be quick. Animals weren't like people. They didn't understand pain. *Now!* He screamed along with the horse as he dug down quickly with the knife and tore the flattened bullet out.

Eagle screamed and threw him sprawling into the sand. The stallion kicked and reared and bucked and started to run away from the light of the fire. Jumping to his feet, dropping the knife, Sundance yelled at the horse to hold up. There was no friendship in the shouted command. Now they were master and servant, no more. Eagle stopped abruptly, lathered with whitening sweat, shuddering with terror.

"Stay, boy!" Sundance ordered as he sawed at shotgun shells with the knife. The knife went through one shell, then another, and he spilled gunpowder into his hand. The wound in the stallion's neck had to be cauterized, had to be closed, to stop the bleeding. Otherwise, Eagle would die.

The firelight was reflected in the great animal's liquid, now distrustful eyes as Sundance walked close, talking softly in Cheyenne, the gunpowder in the palm of his hand. There would be sharp, burning pain when he smeared the gunpowder, but he knew the stallion wouldn't buck and run until he touched a match to the soggy mess of powder and blood.

"Easy, big horse," Sundance said quietly, getting closer. The gunpowder was in one hand, a wood match and a flat stone in the other.

His hands were sweating and he closed his fist

until the gunpowder was rolled into a damp ball. "Take it easy, horse," he said quietly. "It'll be over in a minute."

The stallion's eyes were still distrustful, but there was no movement, no panic, while Sundance came closer and closer. Sundance's voice was soft but firm, telling the great horse to trust him.

He struck the match on the stone and waved it back and forth so Eagle could see that it was just a match. The animal whinnied but held still at Sundance's command.

"Trust me, boy," Sundance said, slapping the damp wad of gunpowder into the wound, pushing hard, and touching the match to it at the same time.

There was a dull, soft flash and a scream from Eagle as the gunpowder flared and burned itself deep into the wound. Sundance was thrown back and had to roll hard to keep from being thrown into the fire. Eagle kicked at him again and ran into the darkness.

Dusting sand from his clothes, Sundance got up and waited for a while. Even when you doctored an animal for its own good, it didn't understand. The smart ones did after a while. Sundance was tired, and he put on a pot of coffee to see what it could do for him.

"Come on back, boy," he called out more than once while the coffee was cooking. "You'll be all right now, boy. Come on back."

In the darkness he heard a whinnying sound, and he said again, "Come on back, Eagle. You'll be all right now."

The great horse walked into the firelight shyly, and Sundance said in English, "You'll be wanting some water now, boy. I don't know what grass there is here, but you'll have water."

Eagle whinnied before he came up and pushed Sundance in the side with his frosted snout.

After two days of resting the horse, Sundance rode down out of the hills without seeing anything to shoot at. It was hot on the flatlands. He knew the two-day delay might have put Hatch far past Rankin City.

Eagle looked all right, but Sundance wasn't taking any chances. He stopped frequently to water the animal, looking for good grazing wherever he went.

Early on the morning of the third day he saw Rankin City in the distance, a small town set down in the middle of the plain.

It was getting on toward noon when he reached the town. He passed a meeting house as he rode in. It had once been a barn, but the preacher had given it a coat of white paint and stuck a cross on the roof. The wooden arm for hoisting baled hay was still in place. A rope hung from the hoist, and there was a dead man at the end of it, swinging and turning in the wind. Around the dead man's neck was a crudely lettered cardboard sign. It read:

BE GOOD OR BE GONE.

It looked like somebody in Rankin City had a sense of humor.

For so early in the day Rankin City seemed a right lively place. The town had three saloons, all going full blast, with player pianos tinkling, and the clamor of rough conversation. The third saloon had a real piano and a real player. The piano was missing some notes. Either that or the player didn't know what he was doing.

There was even a two-storey hotel, with loungers on the porch, spitting and smoking. They watched while Sundance rode on down to the biggest saloon and hitched Eagle at the rack out front. Sundance pushed through the swinging doors, into the smoke and the whiskey smell and the noise.

A mob at the bar was keeping three barkeeps busy. Over past the tables poker and faro and roulette were taking in money as fast as men could lay it down.

The bartender who gave Sundance a beer used a wooden paddle to slice off the head. He looked at Sundance, at his copper skin and yellow hair, but didn't say anything. The beer was good and it was cold. He drank it and ordered another.

About a dozen whores were hustling the drinkers at the bar. Upstairs a balcony ran along the back wall, and off it were the rooms the saloon girls used to entertain their customers—the cribs. Men and girls kept going up and down the stairs.

A whore came up and stood next to Sundance. "Buy me a drink?" she said.

"Sure," Sundance said, motioning to one of the bartenders.

The whore knocked back her drink of cold tea passing as whiskey. She had frizzy blond hair and bad teeth. Apart from the teeth she wasn't bad-looking.

"You're new in town," she said. "You're Indian, ain't you?"

"More or less."

"I knew I'd never seen you before. I know everybody in this town."

The bartender gave the girl another drink without being asked. Sundance put money on the bar.

"What do they call you?"

"Sundance. Jim Sundance."

Sundance looked around as a tall, skinny man in a black coat and hat repeated it. He had a long, mournful face with scooped out cheeks. He had a yellow face and long yellow teeth and his arms were long and awkward. The walnut-butt of his six-gun made an odd contrast with the black minister's coat.

"Seems I heard that name before," he said to Sundance.

"Is he somebody famous, Preacher?" the whore asked.

"Take yourself away for a while, girl," the man called Preacher said, "while me and this gentleman have ourself a chin-wag."

He said to Sundance, "They call me Preacher Carlson. You want another beer?"

"Sure," Sundance said.

He knew something about this Preacher Carlson, and there was nothing to be gained by not talking to him. Twenty years back Carlson had been one of the deadliest gunfighters in the whole Southwest until he was ambushed in an alley but lived through it, and got religion. People said he knew the Bible by heart, backward and forward, and he was still a killer. Looking at Carlson, Sundance didn't doubt it for a minute. This man, getting on in years now, had tamed some of the wildest towns in the West.

"I don't favor beer myself," Preacher Carlson said. "Gives me gas on the stomach and keeps me on the run."

The Preacher ordered whiskey.

He had long loose ears with long lobes, and they gave him a mulish look. "You got yourself quite a reputation, Mr. Sundance," he said.

"So have you, Preacher," Sundance said. "Last time I was in Fort Griffin it was quiet as a church."

"Well, sir, there's nothing better than a nice, quiet town. I aim to do the same for this town. I always say people ought to be able to have a good time without shooting up the place. Not to mention each other. That's how the town fathers feel, and that's why I'm here. What people do in other places don't mean beans to me. I'm no regular lawman so a man can be wanted in three states and I'll let him be as long as he keeps the peace in Rankin City."

"You putting me on notice, Preacher?"

"Hell no, Mr. Sundance. I was just talking, making conversation, as they say. A lot of important citizens in this town got their start on the far side of the law and want to go respectable. That means the shooting and the killing has to stop. I mean to stop it. With the help of the Good Lord, of course."

"Be good or be gone," Sundance said.

"Oh, you saw that. Poor misguided man, God rest his immortal soul. Nobody can say I didn't take him aside and warn him to mend his ways. 'Luther, I said, you're headed straight for perdition if you don't stop beating up the whores. It's no way for a grown man to behave, and I'd take it kindly if you'd quit doing it.'

Preacher Carlson drank his whiskey in one gulp, and poured another.

"You think he'd listen to good advice. No, sir, not Luther Kingman. Not only did he not stop beating the whores, he killed one of them the next time he got crazy drunk. Beat the poor woman to death with a bottle. Anything but that would have been a simple shooting offense. Killing a woman called for hanging, so Luther got hung. Now, Mr. Sundance, if you don't mind my asking—what would your business be in this town?"

Sundance knew that Preacher Carlson had two brothers who traveled with him all the time. They were just as fast, just as folksy, and just as deadly.

"I came here to kill a man named Hatch," he said quietly. "He robbed me of my gold and did his best to kill me. I worked hard for that gold, Preacher. Came by it honestly."

"No matter to me how you got it. You could have robbed a mine for all I care. Only you won't do any killing here. Kill anybody here, Mr. Sundance, and you'll keep Luther Kingman company. I'm telling you that the nicest way I know how."

"No offense, Preacher," Sundance said. "You know this man Hatch?"

"I know him. Seems a nice enough man, though you wouldn't agree, of course. Used to spend a lot of time here, when he wasn't away on business. What his business is I couldn't say. If he tries to kill you, he'll get the same as Luther got. I don't play favorites, Mr. Sundance. If you two want to square off, do it far far away."

"I get your point," Sundance said.

Carlson gave a creaky laugh that showed all his yellow teeth. "I think you and me are going to get along just fine. Nothing like a man who understands the other man's point of view. Drink your beer and have a good time in Rankin City. All this talk of shooting people makes a man doubt the goodness in human nature. You want me to send the girl back. If you don't fancy her, there's plenty more."

"No thanks, Preacher, I got to put up my horse."

Sundance was turning away from the bar when Hatch walked in. There was a bandage around his left arm.

"Well, if it isn't Sundance," he said.

18

"Somebody shoot you, Hatch?" Sundance asked.

Hatch walked over to the bar, and the Preacher moved away from it. "That's right," Hatch answered. "Some feller with a sawed-off. Nothing serious, just a trifle stiff. How's everything with you?"

"The same," Sundance said. "I'm still looking for a man."

"You found him."

"You wouldn't want to take a ride out of town a mile or so? We could settle our business there."

Hatch spoke for the benefit of the drinkers at the bar. "You see this half-breed here. Says I stole his gold. Where in hell would a half-breed get any gold? Now he wants me to ride out of town with him. Not a chance of me doing that. Some of you knew the boys that used to ride with me. Remember Ben Curley? This half-breed killed old Ben with that hatchet. Came at him from behind and split his skull. He killed the others too. Not face to face, like a man. The sneak way is how he done it. I ain't going to ride anywheres with a killer like him."

Preacher Carlson spoke up. "How'd you get that arm, Hatch?"

"The half-breed lay in ambush for me with a sawed-off. Blasted at me with both barrels. If I hadn't heard the hammers going back and dodged behind a rock, I'd be a dead man now. You don't believe me! Take a look at this!"

Hatch unwrapped the bandage on his left arm. There were three buckshot wounds, ugly and red. Hatch showed them off for the crowd, then put the bandage on again.

"I'll take care of this breed in my own way, in my own time," Hatch said.

"Not here you won't, sonny. You got me in front of you, my two brothers behind you." The Preacher stood still, his right hand close to his gun.

Two men in black, some years younger than the Preacher, stood in the doorway with shotguns in their hands. They didn't say anything.

"I just had a talk with your friend here," the Preacher said to Hatch. "Now I'm giving you the same good advice. You and this man have a quarrel, take it out of town."

Hatch said, "Anybody can talk big with two shotguns to back him up."

"I don't need any shotguns to back me. You want to try me, now's the time to do it."

"Hell, Preacher, I don't want any trouble with you." Hatch had a mean temper, but he knew the Preacher's reputation.

"That's the spirit, Mr. Hatch," the Preacher said. "You don't want any trouble with anybody. Not here you don't. Anyway, you got a bad arm. Now I got an even better idea. Why don't me and my two brothers and their two shotguns escort you to the city limits. I'll say it plain—you two men ride out and don't ever come back."

"Suits me," Sundance said, and started for the door. It was going better than he had hoped. He'd be waiting for Hatch when the Carlson brothers made him see the light. "So long, Preacher."

"Be seeing you, Mr. Sundance," the Preacher said.

Hatch turned and yelled at Sundance, "I'll get you good, you stinking half-breed. You ain't going to do me like you done the others!"

"Wait, Sundance," Preacher Carlson called out. Then he looked at Hatch. "You just can't keep your big mouth shut, can you, sonny. You have to keep mouthing off, no matter what. You had your chance to ride out in peace. Now you don't have that chance. I'm taking it back, and if you don't like it, you know what you can do."

"I'm leaving," Hatch said.

"No, sir, you're not," Preacher Carlson said. "I just got a bellyful of your tough talk. You want to fix that man, you say. There he stands. Fix him, if you can. No guns though. That's my rule and it stands. No shooting of guns in my town. I see you're both carrying Bowie knives. That's how you'll do it—with knives."

"Suits me," Sundance said. He unbuckled his gunbelt and put it on the bar with the throwing hatchet. He unsheathed the knife.

Hatch gave his gun to the Carlson brothers. The crowd moved back, and the Carlson brothers held them there, shotguns held waist-high.

"Get on with it," Preacher Carlson said.

Sundance moved out holding the black-bladed knife straight out, edge down.

Hatch jumped forward and tried for an underhand slash at Sundance's wrist. It ripped the shirt, but didn't draw blood. Sundance moved away on the balls of his feet as Hatch came back with an overhand jab. He reached up and blocked it, the two heavy knives clanging loudly in the quiet room. Then he lunged at Hatch's belly, holding the knife straight out like a sword. Hatch jumped back, slashing at Sundance's face as he did so. He missed by inches, then tried for a backhand slash, aiming for the shoulder of the right arm. If he hadn't swung so wildly, he would have cut right to the bone. The razor edge of Hatch's knife opened a thin gash that drew a trickle of blood. Sundance could feel it running down his arm.

Hatch moved in again, the big Bowie weaving in wide circular motions, while Sundance waited for him to come closer. It looked like Burke Hunter had taught him well. The man was a loudmouth braggart, but he knew how to handle a knife. Sundance lunged at Hatch's face, and then made a pass at the underarm. Hatch parried both slashes and drove Sundance back with a fierce, chopping counter-attack. He was fast and agile and confident, and he couldn't help bragging. "Maybe you killed Burke Hunter, but you won't kill me, half-breed." He tried to make Sundance lose his temper. "You're nothing but a mangy, dog-eating scum. A mongrel is all you are! Son of a child raper they chased out of England! You know what your mother was? A smelly cootie-ridden squaw whore! Come on, you half-man! Kill me if you can!"

Hatch was still shouting abuse when Sundance came at him like a cougar. He tried to kick Sundance in the groin while jabbing at his face. Sundance blocked the kick with his thigh, turning fast to avoid the point of the knife. Hatch lost some of his balance by reaching out too far, and Sundance hooked a solid punch to the side of his head. Hatch swerved to one side and kicked again, catching Sundance in the kneecap. A numbing pain ran up his thigh, but he was able to slash through Hatch's boot before he could get his leg out of the way.

Blood gushed out through the slashed leather and Hatch yelled with pain. Blood was still coming from the wound on Sundance's upper arm, the knife handle was slippery in his hand. Quickly he shifted the Bowie to his other hand while he wiped off the blood. He shifted back the knife and bored in again, the blade held straight out. Hatch kicked at him again. Sundance jumped back, his moccasined feet skidding on the spit-slick sawdusted floor. Hatch kicked again and Sundance went down hard on his back. Then Hatch was all over him, stomping and kicking, trying to break his legs with his heavy boots.

The blood from Hatch's leg wound spattered in Sundance's face. He stabbed upward with the knife and stuck the point in Hatch's thigh. It was a short deep wound, and he felt the point strike the bone. He yanked it out, and now Hatch was like a madman, yelling, kicking, and cursing. He jumped high into the air and tried to land on Sundance's face. Sundance rolled away and Hatch staggered when he hit the floor. Moving quickly, Sundance dropped the knife and grabbed Hatch's ankle with both hands and turned it hard. Hatch, yelling with pain, tried to break Sundance's hold. Sundance twisted the ankle again. Hatch broke the hold and went staggering back, giving Sundance time to get back on his feet.

The two men, a few feet apart, stood there, sucking in breath. Hatch was the first to move, and he attacked again, swinging the big knife like a saber, his eyes bright with a killing lust. He came in fast and one of the wild slashes opened Sundance's cheekbone. Blood ran down his face and dripped onto his shirt. Hatch jumped at him, the knife point stabbing at his heart.

Sundance turned the knive and was slashed on the back of the hand. Hatch tried again and Sundance knocked him back with a solid punch in the mouth. It was time to finish, Sundance knew. He pretended to stagger and Hatch roared, thinking he was close to the end. He was. Hatch stopped to roar his triumph. Sundance straightened up and threw the knife as hard as he could. It flashed across the room, straight as an arrow, and Hatch screamed as the blade buried itself up to the haft in his belly. Still screaming, he grabbed the haft of the Bowie with both hands and tried to pull it out. He screamed with pain and terror, and his eyes were crazed with the thought of his approaching death.

The knife wouldn't come out and, still screaming, Hatch tried to grab for Preacher Carlson's holstered gun. Holding his gun butt with one hand, the Preacher shoved him away with the other. Hatch was still on his feet, mumbling, "I swear to God! I swear to God!" His voice rose to a scream, and they all stood there and watched him die. Then, still calling on God, he fell backward, shuddered violently, and lay still.

Sundance walked over to the body and pulled his knife out, and put it back in its sheath without wiping it off. Preacher Carlson took a bottle off the bar and handed it to him. Sundance drank, feeling the raw liquor burning its way down to his belly.

"Get this unfortunate man buried," the Preacher told his two brothers.

They began to drag out the body.

Sundance handed the bottle back to the Preacher, and turned toward the door. The Preacher came after him. Sundance saw Hatch's horse tethered at the rack. He walked over to it and unwrapped the bedroll. There it was—the sack of nuggets so many men had died for.

"That it?" the Preacher asked.

"That's it," Sundance said.

"Well then, my friend, you got no more business in my town. You got your man and you got your gold. Ride out and don't ever come back."

Weary now, sick of killing, Sundance went over to Eagle and pulled himself into the saddle.

"Just one more thing," Preacher said.

"What's that?"

"It's been a pleasure meeting you, Mr. Sundance."

"Likewise, Mr. Carlson."

Two weeks later, after making a long camp while his wounds healed, Sundance rode up to the Hunter ranch. He was leading Eagle to the water trough when Eloise Hunter came out of the house.

"You're back," she said. "I didn't think you would ever be back."

"I'm back."

Looking at her, Sundance decided that she hadn't been too worried about her husband after all.

She stared at him. "Did you . . . ?"

"I found him." Sundance said. "He's dead."

"How did he . . . ?" She shook her head. "Don't tell me. I don't want to know."

"If that's what you want," Sundance said. "Why don't you ask me about the mine. That was the whole idea, wasn't it?"

"How dare you! All right, why pretend? What about the mine? Did you find it?"

"I found it, but that gold belongs to the Apaches. It's sacred to them, but I don't suppose you'd understand."

"To hell with the Apaches! The mine belonged to my husband, and now it belongs to me!"

"The Apaches would dispute that."

"Look, Sundance," Eloise Hunter said, coming up close to him. "You know where the mine is. We could organize a party of men and go back there. As many men as we need, determined and tough, well-armed. I could sell this place to pay for it. I'll raise as much money as it takes. We could be rich, partners, anything you like. For you there would be more than money. If you know what I mean."

Sundance knew. He thought she looked very pretty in the sunlight, the greedy bitch!

"No, Mrs. Hunter," he said. "The gold stays where it is. I didn't bring back your husband, but I did get some gold. I guess some of it belongs to you. But I'll say how much. Now suppose we go in the house and I'll give you your share. Then I'll be riding on."

PRIME TIME — **LB499-2 $1.95**
James Kearney — **Novel**

The book that picks up where *Network* left off . . . The explosive novel of violent power struggles inside a giant television network. The United Television Network. Outside an austere glass facade . . . inside a seething hot bed of ambitious men and women whose motto was "show your rivals no mercy" . . . men and women who would get what they wanted at any cost. (Foil cover)

FLAME IN A HIGH WIND — **LB500-X $1.50**
Jacqueline Kidd — **Adventure**

A Powerful novel of romance and adventure on the high seas. The War of 1812 ended for all but Capt. Denny Poynter. Branded pirate, pursued by British and Americans alike, he fought and plundered his way around the world. But his reckless freedom would be soon jeopardized as his first lady, the sea, gave way to the fiery Renee.

THAT COLLISION WOMAN — **LB501-8 $1.95**
Deidre Stiles — **Novel**

Fleur Collison was known as the most beautiful and wilful woman in all England. The young Englishwoman would return to her ancestral home of Ravensweir despite the fact that it was inhabited by her former lover, now brother-in-law. She was determined to take what she wanted from the world . . . and her sister.

ELENA — **LB502-6 $1.50**
Emily Francis — **Mystery**

The commune on this small Greek island lived a placid life among ancient monuments and clear blue sea until Elena came. They gave her friendship and love. She brought them death.